All he wanted was a meal.
What he got was a fight.

The door burst inward, its latch never having been intended to stop anything the size of Longarm with a full head of steam. As he'd thrown his full weight against the crimson planking, he'd as naturally drawn his .44-40 with his right hand. So as the big galoot inside rolled off the Chinese lady he'd been attacking, Longarm pistolwhipped him before he could get his own side arm, a .45 Walker Conversion, clear of its holster.

The lusty lad of, say, forty was tough as he looked, for even after he'd wound up in a far corner of the tiny room with a lot of blood and at least one tooth dribbling down his unshaven chin, he said mean things about Longarm's mother and kept trying to haul his fool gun out. Longarm booted him in the head so he banged into the wall behind him and flopped over on top of his six-gun in sweet repose.

Longarm turned to the Chinese lady, ticked his hat, and said, "Evening, ma'am. I was just looking for a chop suey parlor."

TABOR EVANS

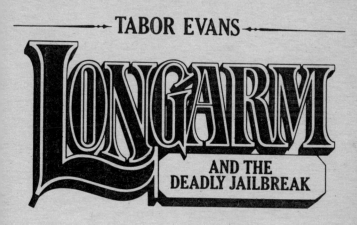

LONGARM

AND THE DEADLY JAILBREAK

JOVE BOOKS, NEW YORK

LONGARM AND THE DEADLY JAILBREAK

A Jove Book/published by arrangement with
the author

PRINTING HISTORY
Jove edition/January 1990

ISBN: 0-515-10212-1

Jove Books are published by The Berkley Publishing Group,
200 Madison Avenue, New York, New York 10016.
The name "Jove" and the "J" logo
are trademarks belonging to Jove Publications, Inc.

PRINTED IN THE UNITED STATES OF AMERICA

10 9 8 7 6 5 4 3 2 1

Chapter 1

Longarm had passed through Arnold Wells many a time aboard the Burlington Line, for the tiny trail town occupied a modest patch of rolling shortgrass range somewhere between Denver and Cheyenne. But until this particular afternoon he'd never been required to really notice the place. The flag stop could be described as about as interesting and about the same color as one of those fuzz balls old maids find under their beds while searching for something more interesting. The trains never stopped at Arnold Wells unless a passenger asked to get off there or a signalman flagged 'em down, polite. And since Longarm had told the conductor he had to get off there, and how come, the Burlington Flier slowed almost to a total stop, depositing Longarm on the sun-silvered loading platform at a dignified trot.

So much for the easy part, he decided, as he came to a halt and put down his heavily laden carpetbag to reach under his tobacco-brown frock coat for a three-for-a-nickel cheroot. For he saw nobody had come over the tracks to meet him, no matter what his own boss, U.S. Marshal Billy Vail, had promised. He struck his horny thumbnail to the head of a waterproof Mex match he packed for such occasions, and got his smoke going as he contemplated the chore of scouting up the town lockup in such a small and strange community. He'd seldom seen a train stop anywhere in broad-ass daylight without so much as a couple of kids drifting over by the tracks. If there was a circus or something else as wondrous drawing the people, he couldn't tell from here. So he picked up his possibles again to draw a bead on a whitewashed church steeple rising against the eastern sky and likely fairly close to the center of town. But then he spied at least half the menfolk a town that size could hold, coming his way all at once and waving everything from buffalo rifles to pitchforks. Their mixed-up growls reminded Longarm of a gathering storm. He put his carpetbag back down and casually got his coattails clear of the grips of his .44-40, riding neither tyro high nor showoff low in its no-bullshit cross-draw rig.

It remained to be seen who they were after. As those in the crowd spotted him, the way he was staring back at them with that big six-gun to back his play, and the don't-mess-with-me smile on his handsome but sort of lived-in tan face, they slowed down some and growled a heap less. An older gent with a brass badge stuck to his black vest and his rawboned fists stuck to the big ten-gauge market gun he carried called a complete halt at easy conversation and point-blank pistol range to ask, in a firm but reasonable tone, who in thunder Longarm might be and had he noticed anyone getting aboard that train just now.

Longarm replied as politely, "I'm U.S. Deputy Marshal Custis Long, working out of the Denver District Court. As you correctly suspected I just dropped off the northbound for Cheyenne. I did not see so much as a yaller dog chase the locomotive out of town. Am I correct in assuming you boys are in hot pursuit of someone at the moment?"

The old-timer with the impressive scatter-gun and mail-order badge replied morosely, "Two or more cold-blooded killers, at least one of 'em of the female persuasion. If nobody even tried to board that train just now, we're sure running out of ideas. Are you by any chance the jasper Denver sent to take Sweet William Allan off our hands?"

Longarm nodded but said, "There was no chance involved. As soon as we got word you'd picked up such a serious federal want on a vagrancy charge, my boss seemed bound and determined I get up here sudden and bring him right back."

He nudged the carpetbag on the platform with the toe of his low-heeled army boot to add, "Chose me by name and insisted I tote along leg irons as well as handcuffs. For Uncle Sam needs the testimony of the young rascal in connection with more serious owlhoot riders, and they say Sweet William can be hard to hold on to."

The older man with the junior badge grimaced and told Longarm, "They should have said it stronger. The occasion of all this turmoil is the latest jailbreak of Sweet William Allan. I am County Deputy Purvis. You may as well call me Pop, everyone else does. Whether you're really the one they call Longarm or not, you're welcome to offer your considered professional opinion, because as of this moment we are just plain stumped!"

Longarm modestly replied, "You got my nickname right, and some say I'm at least as smart as most of the crooks they send me out to bring in. But I've found it

3

best to keep my opinions to myself until I have some notion as to what might or might not have transpired. You boys have considerable advantage on me when it comes to even guessing where your busted-open jail might be from here."

Pop Purvis nodded and pointed in the general direction of the church steeple with his gun muzzle, even though he insisted, "The cuss and his confederates can't be *there* now."

Another voice in the crowd chimed in with, "They ain't nowhere else in town, neither. We've hunted for 'em high and we've hunted for 'em low, and there can't be a hundred hiding places in town even if you count the chicken coops and crappers."

Another would-be manhunter explained, "Sweet William busted out, or his pals busted him out, just as everyone but the two deputies left to guard him was washing up for suppertime. You can see for yourself the sun's still up and there's nothing but shortgrass to hide behind for miles around."

Pop Purvis waved his gun barrel for silence and told Longarm, "The dulcet sounds they made getting Sweet William out of that securely locked patent cell drew considerable attention for miles around, and the whole infernal town ain't a quarter mile across. I made it from my back porch to the jail house in less than five minutes, probably no more than three. Other boys coming from every direction joined me there just about as sudden. But it was all over by then. Two deputies on the floor in front of a gaping cell door, and that's all there was to it at the site of the escape. The mystery ain't how the slippery son of a bitch busted out, Longarm. It's where he went *after*! Anyone can see how one or more confederates just came in and shot poor Dave Rice and Proddy Bob Trevor down like dogs. If we're right about

4

the strange and sort of pretty young gal some say they've seen around town of late, we can even account for the way they got the drop on a couple of my best men. But, damn it, the gunplay brung everyone within earshot to their doorsill or at least their window and . . . Damn it to hell, it just ain't *possible* to ride or, hell, *walk* out of town in broad daylight without some damned body spotting you and being able to tell the infernal law which way you went!"

Longarm hefted his possibles and suggested mildly, "The place I generally commence tracking from is the place the trail had to have started, Deputy Purvis."

The older lawman shrugged and said, "Call me Pop. We'll be proud to show you our swell new jail house, Longarm. They assured us it was escape-proof. Only, all we have now to show for all that money is one hell of a mess to clean up!"

The town lockup of Arnold Wells was no more unusual than the other frame buildings lining either side of the one main street running east from the railroad tracks. All of them had been thrown up cheap but strong enough to take the winter wolf winds out this way. Desperados and even drunken trail hands had been known to kick more serious than the wind at wooden walls, so the otherwise wooden structure had been provided with a row of four boilerplate bolt-together patent or mail-order cells, each barred floor to ceiling with one-inch rods of pretty good vanadium steel. As Pop Purvis led him back to the cell block, bidding his other manhunters to stay out front for now, Longarm could see nobody had bothered to even scratch the gray-green paint off the bars. The door to the second cell from the left gaped wide, the key still in the lock with a big ring holding other keys dangling from it. Longarm asked and Pop told him, "Proddy Bob would have had them keys, on him or more likely in the desk drawer yonder."

Longarm retraced his steps to where the big battered desk stood stolidly in the center of the open space, closer to the front door. The bentwood chair that had once stood behind it lay on its side in a far corner. Longarm didn't ask why. There were gobs of gore and blobs of brain tissue still drying on the shot-up bulletin board behind the desk. There was a big sticky spot on the floor near a gun rack on the far wall facing the patent cells. The holes shot in the gun rack and its contents weren't as obvious until one sort of wondered why someone hadn't cleaned all the rusty crud off that otherwise shiny maple and Parkerized steel. He asked Pop Purvis which of his men had been found dead where. The older lawman said, "Dave Rice went down by the gun rack. He wasn't reaching for a long gun when he died, though. He got hit from the front, with number-nine buckshot judging from the way it tore him up."

He pointed at the messier bulletin board to add, "Proddy Bob must have got it as he was rising behind yonder desk. He got hit with pistol balls and a full charge of buck, fired point-blank. You have to understand something about Proddy Bob Trevor, Longarm. I left him in charge of the prisoner at suppertime because we never named him Proddy Bob for being asleep in the saddle."

Longarm nodded soberly at the overturned chair in the corner and said, "I figured they'd warned you boys, the same way they warned us. Sweet William got his own handle by behaving nothing like he looked. But let's study on how someone else, not him, might have gotten the drop on two picked deputies *expecting* trouble."

Pop Purvis nodded grimly and replied, "You're

damned-A they were expecting trouble. I warned 'em the young rascal we'd taken at first for a saddle tramp with no visible means and a sassy attitude was in pure truth a known associate of the James and Younger Gang and a famous escape artist in his own right. I told both my boys not to let even a lawyer in to talk to the two-faced rascal when I was out of this infernal office! But did they listen? Lord, you should have seen how tore-up we found 'em, Longarm. They're getting cleaned up for burial at the cabinetmaking and undertaking establishment if you want to look 'em over, by the way."

Longarm grimaced and said, "I'll take your word they're both dead, and the coroner's report should satisfy Billy Vail if ever he wants to pick nits about it. Knowing how one or more killers came in here packing shotguns as well as six-guns, and won, is the question before the house as far as I'm concerned."

Pop Purvis nodded and said, "I'm ahead of you on that. Some of the other boys have suggested neither Proddy Bob nor Dave Rice were helpless orphans. As anyone can read it, they were spaced out a good two or three yards apart, with old Bob seated at the desk and Dave by yonder gun rack. Both were wearing their own guns when we scraped 'em off this floor not long ago. So we're talking about someone mighty good, if he or she was even visible."

Longarm shot a glance at the glass windows to either side of the door. It was well after suppertime indeed, by now. But it was still bright enough outside to see colors and the sun would have been a heap brighter between four and five P.M., when most country folk ate supper. He said, "I don't go along with anyone impossible to see in broad-ass daylight. I've run across this same puzzle before and, so far, it's never been an invisible haunt. A gal I used to be fond of taught me some stage magic,

7

up to the Pine Ridge Reserve, when we were having trouble with a pesky medicine man. You'd be surprised how simple some impossible happenings really work, once you savvy the way you were hoodwinked."

Pop Purvis grumbled, "No I wouldn't. I ain't superstitious. I'm only bewildered. I know we've all missed something that was no doubt there for all the world to see, if only the damned old world had been looking."

Then he pointed at the door with his own shotgun muzzle to demand, "Suppose you tell me how you'd go about striding through that one door there, with Proddy Bob watching from behind this desk here, and good old Dave standing yonder, by the gun rack, with his own gun riding loose in its holster!"

As Longarm traced imaginary lines with his iron-gray eyes, the older lawman continued, "Say the killer or killers just busted in, guns drawn. Don't you reckon either Dave or Bob would at least *try* for their own side arms?"

Longarm shrugged and said, "Let's set that part aside, for now. There's never a bronco that couldn't be rode, never a rider that couldn't be throwed, and never a gunslick that couldn't be beat to the draw by somebody slicker. I think you're missing the *really* impossible part, Pop."

But Purvis shook his head and replied, "No I ain't. I was the one who just told you the whole damned town heard the gunplay and came running from every damn direction about the same time!"

Longarm mentally paced off the distance between that gaping cell door and the desk and overturned chair before he decided aloud, "Nobody's that fast. Leaving aside the fact that it takes a second or longer to blow two grown men away, it takes even longer to search for that key ring, get over to that cell door, and figure the right key. That one door faces the main street, where you say gents all up and down it ran to their own doors or windows at the first dulcet sound of a needlessly noisy jailbreak, Pop."

Purvis nodded but said, "It's been agreed the commotion consisted of at least two shotgun blasts and considerably more pistol peppering, but how come you call that needless, Longarm? Dave Rice was no slouch in a firefight and Proddy Bob was downright dangerous!"

Longarm shook his head and insisted, "The killer or killers got the drop on both before the first shots were fired, unless you were mistaken about neither deputy hitting the floor with his own gun even halfway out. So either those shotgun blasts or a few discreet pistol shots should have done it. No offense, but the tale you all tell sounds to me as if the intent of all that noise was misdirection."

Pop asked Longarm to run that by him again, slower. So Longarm explained, "You all heard shots. More shots than were needed to drop two men, even good ones. You all naturally assumed gunplay somewhere near the center of town meant a holdup, jailbreak, or whatever because that's the usual scene of such activity. But study back just a mite and tell me true whether you were standing smack out front with those guns going off in here, or whether you could have heard the gunplay from some distance and just *supposed* it had something to do with a locked-up outlaw, the only one in town, as far as you or anyone else knew."

Pop Purvis cocked a half-convinced eyebrow. Then he scowled and objected, "Hold on. I said I was washing up on my back porch, a city block and around the corner away from yonder front door. So I could have been mistaken about the direction the sounds of gunshots were coming from. Only I wasn't. When I came busting in here a few short moments later this very room was blue with gunsmoke and the blood and brains spattered all about were still dripping."

Longarm pointed out, "The goo ain't dried out all the way yet, and you can still taste brimstone in here with no cross ventilation worth mention. I'm still working on just when and how your deputies died. There's no way they went down in that fusillade that brought you and so many others running. The only way Sweet William and his rescuers got out that one and only door was *earlier*, before anyone heard all those gunshots."

As the older lawman stared after him thundergasted, Longarm strode to the door, threw it open, and pointed with his jaw at an alley entrance just across the way, saying, "Let's not jump to conclusions before we scout it some, but someone firing up at the sky a lot over yonder could just turn around and stroll away after pulling a hundred eyes or more to swell view of this jail house, Pop. Let's go see if they were smart enough to police their own brass."

As they both stepped back out into the gloaming, the sun having almost set by this time, the others they'd left hanging in suspense outside crowded in around them until Pop Purvis yelled, "Calm your fool selves, damnit. Me and Longarm have it figured out more possible, now. Don't nobody walk ahead of us as we cross over to yonder shortcut through to Morpeth Street."

Nobody did, but a young cuss dressed more cow than most fell in beside Purvis to point out, "It'll soon be too dark out on the range for tracking, Pop." Purvis replied in a disgusted tone, "You just mount up and ride out after the rascals, then. Let us know as soon as you cut the right trail on summer-kilt and wind-cured shortgrass stubble, spread by hundreds of loving hoods over adobe soil baked hard as your head!"

10

By this time Longarm's long strides had taken him across Main Street. Purvis told the others not to follow as he entered the alley a few paces behind Longarm. The overhead sky was now lavender and the alley shadows were deep purple. But Longarm knew what he was looking for, and as soon as he spotted it he dropped to one knee, plucked his prize from the darker cinder dust, and rose to hold it out to Pop in his gritty palm, saying, "Sixty-six shotgun. Extraction scratches still fresh." He held his hand up to his mustache, sniffed, and added, "Fired within hours at most. Do you folk hunt many ducks down this particular alley, Pop?"

Purvis told him not to rub it in as he bent over to pick up a smaller spent shell and sniff it, growling, "Forty caliber, fired as recent. You're sure making me feel dumb, Longarm. But whether we heard shots coming from here or yonder jail house, ain't we discussing unusual guns as well as unusual gunshots?"

Longarm took the pistol brass from Purvis and held it up to such light as there was before he replied, "We could be talking about a Le Mat conversion, Pop. I don't know if they still manufacture such monstrous weapons, but when they did, they did so over in France, where they measure ammo different. Neither of these shells have any brands stamped into their brass. Likely the product of some small-time gunsmith, making up wildcat rounds on special order."

He put both in a coat pocket, adding, "I'm impounding 'em as federal evidence. There's an outside chance such shells have been noticed by others riding for other offices, and if ever we can get a line on who makes such brass, and who he sells it to—"

"You're getting way the hell out ahead of me!" Purvis protested. "What in thunder is a Le Mat and how did French gunsmiths get into this?"

11

Longarm bent to pick up yet another .40 caliber shell and pocket it as he replied, "A growing boy your age should have seen a Le Mat by this time, Pop. They were imported in numbers during the war back East, before anyone noticed how expensive a Le Mat revolver was to run, next to cheaper Connecticut Yankee products such as Colt Arms of Hartford cranks out. The first Le Mats were cap and ball. That made for a really tedious loading chore, with the big pissoliver chambered for nine bullets and a shotgun charge."

Purvis whistled and said, "You're right. Sounds like a mighty messy weapon to shoot or get shot by! But if it loaded cap and ball, with no brass shells—"

"They worked better converted to more modern ammo by any halfway decent gunsmith," Longarm cut in, picking up another spent .66 and pocketing it. "I said they were expensive as well as clumsy artillery. Two regular six-guns don't weigh much more, together, and throw as much metal once you study on it. The very few owlhoots still flourishing Le Mats or other such single-shot hoglegs do so more to scare folk than anything else. Albeit in this case they might have found it easier to throw down on your deputies with shotguns disguised as pistols than vice versa."

Pop Purvis took off his battered Stetson, scratched his short-cropped and gray-thatched scalp, and decided, "You'd best take charge of this whole infernal investigation, then. For I'll be switched with snakes if I can make heads or tails of what you just now said! First you tell me some asshole just shot up the sky, from this alley, to make us think we were hearing gunshots from the jail house, and then you tell me they *did* gun both them poor boys across the way with big old guns from frogland and— Jesus H. Christ, Longarm, what really took place around here this very afternoon?"

Longarm got out a fresh cheroot and lit it, staring soberly up and down the alley in vain before he admitted sheepishly, "I don't know. We got to eat the apple a bite at a time. It gets one bite out of the way if we allow they somehow got Sweet William out and murdered your two deputies sometime *before* you all heard all those shots and came running. That accounts for how come nobody saw anyone leaving the jail house right after they heard the shots. They'd already left and the shots were fired from here instead of there. Then all they had to do was stroll out the far end on to... Morpeth Street, you said?"

Purvis nodded and told him, "Residential street. No place to hide once you leave the far end of this alley." But then he had to tag on after Longarm as the younger but more thorough lawman strode away from Main Street and its saloons and railroad stop, observing, "You ask folk whether they've noticed anyone trying to hide. Then you say whether there's anyplace for 'em to hide or not."

By the time they'd come out the far end some of the other townsmen of Arnold Wells had screwed up the courage to follow. But at least the crowd had shrunk to no more than a dozen as Longarm paused to stare up and down the narrower dirt-paved street, noting most of the structures in sight seemed to be modest-sized private houses of frame or sod. Here and there a summer-withered garden tried to grow behind a sun-bleached picket fence. Nobody had ever even tried to plant a tree along Morpeth Street. So even though the light was tricky by this time, Longarm could see how unlikely it was that anyone dashing out of that alley could have found any handy place to hide, without an out-and-out invite.

First things coming first, Longarm pointed his cheroot at the frame house directly across the way to ask

13

Pop Purvis who might or might not own such a grand view smack down the alley they'd just come out of. Purvis said, "That's the Morpeth place. Regina Morpeth would never in this world aid and abet dangerous strangers from out of town!"

Longarm didn't ask how a local property owner might feel about dangerous fellow townsfolk. He started to cross over as he said, "Her bay window covers the alley exit mighty fine, though. Tell me more about the lady, starting with how she got her own street named after her, Pop."

Purvis grimaced and said, "You got that bass ackwards. Morpeth Street was laid out before Regina Morpeth was born. You see, Arnold Wells was settled back before the war by lapsed Mormons who didn't feel up to following Brigham Young over the Shining Mountains into what was then part of Mexico, whether it was all desert or not. Everyone who wasn't related to Captain Arnold, the leader of the party, was a Morpeth, Prudhoe, Purvis or Rothbury, so they naturally felt free to name things here in town after themselves."

Longarm nodded and said, "We'll get to the townsfolk along Purvis Street later, Pop. I didn't know you were a Saint."

Purvis shrugged and replied, "I ain't. I told you we'd decided the Mormon Faith was too complicated for us. I was just a kid at the time, of course, so my elders did most of the thinking for me, but—"

"What time are we talking about?" Longarm cut in with a thoughtful frown. "The late Brigham Young wasn't leading his people into the Promised Land quite as early as Moses might have, you know. I wasn't there, but we are talking thirty years and change ago, right?"

Purvis nodded but asked, "What's that got to do with Proddy Bob and poor old Dave Rice getting buried tomorrow in the here and now? I wasn't old enough to vote, and neither Miss Regina nor that prisoner nor my two dead deputies had anything to say about the founding of this town, the naming of its points of interest, or— What *are* we hunting for, damn it?"

Longarm said, "Sign. You can't hunt nothing before you cut some sign, Pop." Then he swung open the gate to march on over to the front steps of the Morpeth house on Morpeth Street.

Miss Regina Morpeth must have been watching from behind the lace curtains of her big front window. For she swung open her front door before Longarm could twist the doorbell handle, and he found it hard to concentrate on escaped prisoners he'd never seen in the flesh as he considered how much flesh the petite ash-blonde in the doorway was exposing, even though she was holding her red kimono shut with one coy hand. She'd likely lost the sash to it in her recent travels. She blinked at Longarm sort of suspiciously as well as sleepy eyed, spotted Pop Purvis just behind him, and murmured, "Evening, Uncle Cyrus, what on earth's going on out yonder? Men keep riding by, and I could swear I heard fireworks earlier. Wasn't the Fourth of July a good spell back?"

Pop Purvis soothed, "We're well into August and it wasn't fireworks you heard, exactly. Regina, this stranger is U.S. Deputy Long and this ain't a social call. We've reason to suspect somebody fired off a mess of shots at the far end of that alley across the way, before running out this end in full view of your bay window. Your turn, honey."

She blinked up at them, looking more confused albeit wider awake now, and that seemed to remind her she was standing in an open doorway with an almost open kimono on. So she answered, "We'd better talk about it

15

inside, gentlemen. I don't know if what I have to tell you could have anything to do with gunplay, but at least I can coffee and cake you."

They followed her back to her kitchen. She waved them both to seats around her raw pine kitchen table and turned her back on them to fluster at her big cast-iron range while Pop Purvis filled her in on the jailbreak. Longarm was less surprised to discover everyone in town seemed sort of related to one another than he was at the fact that she claimed to be a spinster gal who wrote poetical books for fun and profit. He was sure, from where he sat, that she let that kimono hang open all the way, on the far side, as she used both hands to heat up the pot and cut the cake. Whether she did or not he felt sure that she had to be single of her own free will. Good-looking gals who owned their own property were considered a real prize in these parts, even if they did appear to sleep mighty late, or early, depending on what she'd been doing asleep upstairs at the time of the bust out. He didn't consider that any of his own business. But he did feel it polite to ask her attractive rear view just what it was she might be fixing to tell them, once it got sort of obvious she seemed to need some prodding.

She clutched more modestly at the front of her kimono as she turned to serve them, slow and sort of clumsy with the one hand she was free to use in front of men she didn't know in the biblical sense. As she did so she confided, "There may be nothing to it, Deputy Long, but as my uncle or anyone in town can tell you, I've been known to let out rooms upstairs in the past."

As she placed a handsome wedge of sponge cake before him, Longarm asked how far in the past and how come. So she confided, "I found myself a little short of money right after my dear widowed mother died and left

16

me some unpaid bills as well as this property."

Her uncle smiled approvingly up at her to tell Long-arm, "She paid off a hundred pennies to the dollar. Her mother was my sister, you see."

Regina fluttered her long lashes modestly as she poured the coffee, telling Longarm, "I'm more independent these days, ever since some of my poetry's been published back East. I'd like to show you some of my printed works, if you've the time."

He tried to sound sincere as he replied, "Another time, when your uncle and me ain't on the trail of less artistic folk, Miss Regina. You said you might know something about Sweet William's jailbreak, didn't you?"

She sat herself down across from him, and as he noticed to his chagrin how good she was at eating cake and sipping coffee without letting that kimono open all the way, she told him, "There was a young lady, just the other night, pestering me for shelter. She said she needed at least two rooms. One for her and her husband and another for their traveling companion, another man, I think. Though I could be wrong about that."

Longarm told her, "I doubt you're wrong, ma'am. Even one of 'em being female comes as a mild surprise albeit, now that I study on it, a lady of any description could get a heap closer to an armed deputy before he considered going for said arms. What did this mystery woman looked like, Miss Regina?"

The young blonde sighed wistfully and said, "Prettier than I'll ever be, and having allowed that, I hope you won't think I'm being spiteful when I add she didn't strike me as a lady. I'm sure she had her lips and eyelids colored artificial, and I know her hair had been just plain henna-rinsed. And as for her clothes, well, if a lady can't afford real silk there's no shame in wearing

17

cotton, as long as you don't have it mercied shiny to resemble silk!"

Longarm said quietly, "I think they call it mercerized cotton when they shine it so with chemicals, ma'am. It's almost as easy for a gal to change her hair color as it is her duds, no offense. So could we go back over those parts of her that'd look the same no matter when and where a lineup might be held?"

Regina washed some of her own cake down with coffee, frowned as if in concentration, and came up with, "There was something about her looks I didn't like. I'd have never hired her a room even if I'd needed the money and she hadn't mentioned strange men under my roof. But as I think back it's hard to say what made my flesh creep so at the sight of her. Her makeup and flashy summer frock couldn't have been all there was to it. Some of the younger ladies here in Arnold Wells should be ashamed of the way they get gussied up for a Sunday meeting on the green but I still talk to them. As I said, she was very pretty in her own . . . sort of sinister way."

Longarm asked thoughtfully, "Might she have been sort of exotic featured, say sort of Latin or not quite white? Lots of folk are a mite spooked by breeds, without knowing just why they should be."

The obviously Anglo-Saxon gal across the table from him shook her blonde head and said, "It was nothing like that. She looked as plain American as you or me but— Oh, I just remembered, she said her name was Barbara, Barbara Allan."

Before Longarm could respond Pop Purvis gasped, "Thunderation and talk about gall! Everyone in town who considered it at all knew the prisoner we were holding for you was Sweet William *Allan*, Longarm!"

18

Longarm didn't answer, his eyes half closed in reflection as he softly hummed an old song well known of old in the hills of his native West by God Virginia. Pop Purvis stared at him as if he'd just commenced jerking off. But the poetic Regina brightened and let out a delighted little laugh. Then she started singing along, and the next thing poor Pop Purvis knew the two of them were singing, as a fair duet:

> " 'Twas in the merry month of May
> When maple buds were swelling
> Sweet William lay him down to die
> For love of Barbara Allan."

They might have sung more. The old North Country ballad went on for at least as many verses as *Riley's Daughter*. But Pop Purvis banged on the table with his fork to demand, "How did we get us an infernal singing festival going here, you infernal young tweety birds?"

So they both laughed, sharing something with their eyes that hadn't been there before, and Longarm told the puzzled old cuss, "Lord knows whether Sweet William Allan's real name is Smith or Jones, but it's stretching the laws of chance way out of shape for a strange gal to show up in a town this size using Barbara Allan as her real name. I'll ask her when I catch her whether she was trying to be funny or picked the name out of her girlhood memories without considering where it came from. The point is that we've got a few more bites out of the apple. Sweet William's pals used a pretty gal to give them an edge on your deputies at the jail house. The details ain't half as important as when they done it, and the fact they were scouting for someplace to hide, smack here in town, after they done it!"

19

Pop's jaw dropped. It was his young niece who protested, "They *can't* still be here in Arnold Wells, Deputy Long! Who on earth would take strangers in right after a jailbreak, for heaven's sake?"

She looked upset as well as worried. So he tried to keep his own voice calm, considering, as he told them both, "That works better than invisible outlaws riding out of town in broad daylight. Now that I see how tightly knit your little community is, I can go along with your notion nobody would willingly shelter the killers of two local boys, Miss Regina. But consider your own earlier words as I drag you both back over them. You said that mysterious young gal approached you for rooms to let *before* anyone made move-one to get Sweet William out of jail. As I read the timing, it must have been right after Pop, here, picked the young rascal up!"

Old Purvis nodded and said, "We wired your boss, Billy Vail, as soon as we noticed how swell our vagrant's innocent-looking features matched up with all them federal Wanted fliers. So, right, that sassy gal must have blown into town around the same time and— What if she was with him all the time?"

Longarm shrugged and said, "She couldn't have been too close to him when you picked him up on suspicion. But say they were just passing through, he got arrested, she needed time to send for some help and a place for all of them to hide out, after, and we're sure wasting a heap of time on the dead past!"

Draining the last of his cup, Longarm rose to his feet, saying, "That was swell, ma'am. But as anyone can see, the outlaws ain't here in your kitchen or out on the lone prairie, either, unless there's been a rash of sudden blindness in these parts."

Pop Purvis got up as well, of course, but asked just

where they were going. So Longarm told him, "Skunk hunting. They've got to be hiding out right here in town. It sounds a lot easier once you consider they've got guns, and some poor homeowner we haven't talked to yet might not even be alive at this late date!"

Chapter 2

Some bitched that the search felt ever tenser as the evening shades grew ever darker and they had fewer and fewer places to search. As a more experienced lawman, Longarm had naturally started out tense as the situation called for, knowing the disadvantages he was working under. For while Pop Purvis and his informally deputized search parties knew friend from foe, or at least friend from stranger, on sight, Longarm hadn't grown up in this tight-knit bitty trail town, and so he had to hold his fire until someone acted downright ugly, lest he blow away some innocent townsman whose only crime was a surly expression.

Longarm had no idea what Sweet William's rescuers, male or female, looked like. He'd read the descriptions that failed to agree in every detail from one flier to another, and the K.C. office had sent them a sepia-tone blur of two young saddle tramps that might or might not have been Sweet William Allan and Charles Ford, a known associate of the James and Youngers, posing together in Missouri one time. The taller blur was said to be Sweet William. Longarm had been sort of banking on a more formal introduction before they ever had to shoot it out at short notice. So he made sure he had at least a couple of Arnold Wells boys with him each time he eased open a gate to mosey across a dooryard in the uncertain light.

Pop Purvis and a couple of surviving deputies that knew their asses from their elbows had of course assumed command of other sweeps. So once Longarm and his own boys were satisfied nobody they'd elected to check out had any visitors, welcome or otherwise on or about their property, he bought his crew a round of drinks in the corner saloon near the Western Union, and then went there to get some wires off. Pop Purvis had already alerted the county seat about the jailbreak. So the telegraph clerk said he had some urgent messages for old Pop. Longarm finished block lettering his own terse message to Billy Vail before he handed it across the counter and said, "May as well send this night-letter rates. Won't be anyone at my office in the Denver Federal Building at this hour."

The clerk nodded but asked what about the instructions for Pop Purvis from the county sheriff's department. Longarm accepted them, saying, "I have to scout the cuss up in any case, unless I mean to turn in for the night with the bats in your one church belfry."

The clerk didn't argue. He knew Longarm was the lawman helping Purvis track down those jailbreaking sons of bitches. But tracking down Pop Purvis turned out more of a chore than expected. For when he came across a couple of the boys who'd been sweeping another part of town with Pop, they assured him they hadn't caught more than a chill and offered to buy him a drink of medicinal red-eye, lest he come down with the ague, too, now that it was getting so late on the High Plains after sundown.

He said he'd buy them one, another time, and after considering where he'd be if he was the town law, he headed first for the town lockup and, when that didn't work, the cabinetmaker cum undertaker he'd had pointed out to him in passing, earlier that night.

The shop front was shuttered for the night, to nobody's great surprise, but he spied light in the back. So he pounded with his six-gun a spell and, sure enough, a skinny old coot in bib overalls and rolled-up red flannel underwear came to the door to tell him the damned funeral wasn't until ten in the damned morning. But he let Longarm in when he saw the federal badge winking at him through the grimy glass. As he did so, he grumbled, "Don't tell nobody else or they'll all want a look-see, the nosy bastards. What are you after, the cause of death, for God's sake?"

Longarm said, "As a matter of fact, I'm more interested in where your town law might be, alive and apparently itchy footed as all get out. But as long as we're on the subject of those unfortunate deputies and the way they wound up so stiff—"

"Come on back," the part-time mortician cut in. "I was just making 'em presentable for their grand send-off at First Congregational in the morning."

As Longarm followed the older man through the poorly lit but nice-smelling cabinet shop, perfumed by cedar, pine, and other fresh-cut woods, he asked cautiously, "Didn't this town start out as a sort of lost Mormon colony?"

The cabinet- and coffinmaker grunted, "Afore my time, if it was. Most of the folk who get to church at all seem to be Calvinists of the Congregational persuasion. Neither as spoilsport as Baptists nor as odd in their ways as Mormons. I'm a Methodist, myself, so I don't have to go to church at all in Arnold Wells, and to tell the truth I don't suspect the Lord worries all that much about it, neither."

Longarm filed that silently away. His job called for him being nosy about matters that might not be any of his business under other conditions. He figured he could just forget about religion, now that he knew he wasn't dealing with a tight-knit block of anything in particular. But as he followed the old cabinet- and coffinmaker into a more brightly lit but much gloomier workroom, he found himself asking, "Being a Methodist, sir, might you be in a position to tell me whether I'm right about Rice and Trevor both being Welsh names?"

The older man moved around to the far side of the two bodies he had in the center of the room, covered with grimy sheeting save their two waxen faces. He started to ask a dumb question. Then he nodded soberly and said, "As a matter of fact, a lot of Methodists do seem to be Welsh. I think our sect got started some-where near Wales by the Wesley brothers. They wrote *Hark the Herald Angels Sing*, and my people were Dutch in the old country. What are we arguing about?"

Longarm chuckled and said, "Not much, seeing this town can't be party to too many family secrets. It crossed my mind that I've been places in the past where the townsfolk sort of clam up in the presence of the law. This don't figure as one of those times. So I got to go back to the beginning and start from scratch with no easy answers involving a tight little town protecting one of their own against outsiders."

The native of the town, charged with taking care of its dead, regardless of their religion, got back to work

25

with a big soft paintbrush and some dry pink powder as he replied objectively, "The way I heard it, this young cuss riding through left his pony tethered out front of the Pronghorn and got to bragging some on his prowess while he drank a mite unwisely inside."

He swept some obvious face powder away from the one cadaver's hairline as he continued, "It was Dave Rice, here, who thought to have a harmless look-see in the boastful stranger's saddlebags, just in case he was telling the truth about all the ferocious cowhands he'd ridden with in his time. Once Dave found a running iron wrapped indiscreet in dirty socks, well, you came up here to take the sassy young cuss off our hands, didn't you?"

Longarm nodded down at the two dead boys, for neither could have been thirty when they died, and replied, "That's about the size of it. You'd think a traveling man who's held up as many banks as Sweet William Allan would know better than to brag right out about being even slightly sinister. But his yellow sheets have him down for bragging on having screwed Belle Starr and helping Cole, Frank, and Jesse stop the Glendale train, more than once. So I reckon these nice kids arrested the right man. They just failed to recall Sweet William got his nickname from looking like a harmless young asshole."

The undertaker nodded and said, "It's the harmless-looking ones you have to watch out for. They say the Thompson brothers look like liquored-up buffoons and that Billy the Kid could pass for a sissy girl dressed up as a cowboy if he put his mind to it. The doc told me both these boys were hit from the front, point-blank. So the killers must have looked like nothing much as well, right?"

Longarm shrugged and said, "One of 'em might even

26

have been pretty. I'm glad you just mentioned a gent with an M.D. after his name looking these boys over. I take it you have someone here in town authorized to act for the coroner over to the county seat?"

He was told they'd yet to bury anyone at First Congregational without a proper death certificate. Longarm had already figured out both the boys back here were dead. So if medical opinion backed the evidence found at the scene of their killing, there was nothing further for him to do here. He thanked the older townsman for the look-see and left to scout up that infernal old fart, Purvis.

He was told that some old boys saddling up to head on home had just been jawing with Pop and that they'd seen him heading for the lockup when they'd parted friendly. But when Longarm got there the cleanup crew told him he'd just missed Pop. One hand, seeking in vain to get up stale blood with lye water, told Longarm Pop had ducked into that alley across the way, maybe to take a leak. Longarm told them to try lemon juice on bloodstains, if they could get any, and strode out and across to that dumb alley again, feeling dumb as he usually did, running around in circles. But things commenced looking up as he came out the far end to spy the blonde Regina Morpeth engaged in conversation near her front gate. She'd put a more decent dress of summer-weight calico on, seeing how close it was getting to bedtime for the rest of the town, and the young cuss she was jawing with looked vaguely familiar as well as cowhand to Longarm. As he joined them, Regina introduced her late-night caller as Cousin Fred, and as they shook on it Longarm explained he was looking for their older mutual kinsman in order to hand over the instructions from the county seat.

Fred Purvis, as he was called, said he'd be proud to

27

take the wires off Longarm's hands, since he was staying the night at Pop's place and the old man had to get home sooner or later.

But as Longarm started to hand the yellow papers over, Regina reached between them, sort of imperiously to Longarm's way of thinking, and said, "We'd best see what the county wants us to do. Let's all go up under my porch light so we can read them."

Fred Purvis said he didn't think they ought to. Longarm tended to agree but followed her up the steps anyway, as long as it was her notion to open other folk's telegrams.

In the end it turned out less important than expected. The county sheriff didn't want Pop Purvis to do anything in particular as long as he went through the usual motions. The county said it would. They had their own posse out in the unlikely event the vaguely described outlaws paused to carve their initials in anything or anybody. Longarm was too polite to express himself fully in front of a lady when she read him the part about letting the infernal federal government have the infernal case, since it was Uncle Sam, not any county in the state of Colorado, so anxious to try Sweet William on all those federal charges.

Regina, bless her, had the courtesy to call her county sheriff a lazy old silly, and point out that even she could see the murders of poor Dave and Proddy Bob had to count as crimes worth local concern. But as she handed the sheets to young Fred, Longarm soothed, "My department did have first dibs on Sweet William, and he can only hang once, so I reckon your county's being fair as well as practical. They figure the rascals are long gone by now, anyway."

Fred declared in a disgustingly cheerful tone, "I know I'd never let the sun set on myself within a hundred miles of where I'd just shot two whole deputies!"

Longarm raised a dubious eyebrow to reply, "A hundred miles might be stretching it some, but they figure to gain a whole night's lead on us before we can even hazard a guess as to which way they rode." Then he added, half to himself, "That's assuming they rode, of course."

The cousins exchanged glances. Regina asked Longarm, "Are you saying Sweet William and his dreadful Barbara Allan are still hiding out somewhere in town, Deputy Long?"

Longarm shrugged and said, "You told us earlier about a mysterious fake redhead trying to hire room and board for herself and at least two men, right here in town. I failed to hear anyone say she was out to hire three livery mounts or a prairie schooner."

"I told you I turned her down," Regina protested. "Would you like to search my root cellar for the rascals?"

He chuckled and replied, "Not having a search warrant, I have to take your word for it, just as we've had to take the word of all the others on good faith. Nobody owned up to aiding and abetting, but then, who would, if the price was right?"

Young Fred nodded soberly and declared, "I'd best get that notion to Pop along with the county's suggestions about letting you federal lawmen worry about it. I can see you've already started. So good luck, good hunting, and I'll be over at my uncle's if there's anything I can do for you."

They shook on it and young Fred lit out. As Longarm and the blonde watched him fade from sight down the dim-lit side street, he asked and she told him more about her family tree than he'd really wanted to know.

Her cousin Fred was the son of yet another Purvis, making Pop, or Cyrus, uncle to both of them. The four or five families who'd first settled Arnold Wells were so intermarried that it was small wonder they all called their town law Pop. By the time she'd explained all this by her garden gate, the summer night, being a High Plains night, had cooled to where he could feel it, even under his tweed coat, and her summer-weight bodice had to be goosebumping her worse. So he said as much and allowed they'd best call it a day before they both caught their deaths. She told him he was a considerate gent and asked where he was staying in town, in case anyone came looking for him.

He smiled down at her uncertainly and confided, "I still have to work that out. Maybe at the saloon across from the railroad stop. If it was left to me alone I'd just catch the next night train back to Denver and say no more about it. But my boss, Marshal Vail, may have some loose ends for me to tidy up here in Arnold Wells, and he won't get to the office this side of sunrise."

She said, "We'd best talk about it inside, then. There's no hotel at all in town, and you're so right about how nippy it's commencing to get."

He started to object that finding shelter after the saloon shut down could get even tougher. Then he wondered why anyone would want to talk so dumb to a pretty gal living alone. So in no time at all they were back in her kitchen and she was rustling up a spider of scrambled eggs and pork sausage for the two of them. As he sat there fondly watching her do so she reminded him she had said she had more than one extra room upstairs to let. But when he asked how much he'd owe her if he had to stay a night or more, depending on Billy Vail or any break in the case, she told him not to be an old silly and reminded him she was kin to the town law.

30

So he dropped that sordid subject and obeyed her command to hang up his hat and coat, even though she'd only commanded, "If you feel more comfortable that way."

When she served more coffee, strong as an ox and black as a banker's conscience, he was reminded once more about the way the town had been founded by lapsed Mormons. The Latter-day Saints didn't hold with coffee, tea, tobacco or demon rum. As she sat down catty-corner to him and they both dug in, he got more local history out of her. More than he really thought he needed to know, as a matter of fact. For while most folk raised country tended to just eat and get it over with, Regina apparently considered herself more worldly since she'd had some of her poetry published, and she took him up on his few casual questions about her neighbors to lecture him on local history.

It would have sounded duller if she hadn't had such a pleasant voice and amusing way of putting things. But it would have been a heap more interesting to Longarm if it hadn't been such a familiar yarn.

Western towns tended to sprout up more mushroom in appearance than in fact. Like towns anywhere on earth, they had to have reasons to sprout at all. Arnold Wells had preceded the railroad by a few years as a wide spot in the trail from Santa Fe to the South Pass. Its main reason for existing anywhere lay in its name. Captain Arnold and his wagon party of lapsed Mormons had noticed all-year water and one hell of a lot of shortgrass range for the taking, so they'd taken it, shooting off the few pesky redskins who'd objected, and neither the coming of the Goodnight Cattle Trail nor the Burlington Railroad had hurt business worth mention. Longarm washed down some sausage and eggs and remarked he'd noticed their swell Carpenter's Classic bank near the town lockup. When she said that was where she cashed the checks they sent her for her poems, he asked how often it got robbed. She said it never had and suddenly gasped, "Good grief! Is that why you think those outlaws could still be here in town, Deputy Long?"

He put his cup down again, saying, "My folk named me Custis. I don't know why. I'd never done anything mean to them. Anyway, I don't know whether Sweet William and his Barbara Allan are hiding out here in Arnold Wells. If they are, without a good reason, then they have to be so dumb we don't have much to worry about. It can't be midnight yet, so they'd have a good six hours of darkness if they only started walking on foot. If they're still in town come morning, it can be assumed they have a reason. I'll tell you how sensible a reason it was after I figure out what it was."

She poured more coffee, suggesting, "It seems to me just getting Sweet William out of jail by murdering two guards ought to inspire some laying low indeed! You surely don't expect them to rob the bank or anything else on their way out of town, Custis!"

He frowned thoughtfully and mused half to himself, "To tell the pure truth, I can't make heads or tails out of anything that's transpired here to date. We have Sweet William Allan down as a stickup man, not a cow thief. Yet the story goes that he was dumb enough to get drunk in a strange town with a running iron in his saddlebag. I sure wish the arresting officer hadn't wound up so dead. I'd like to ask him why he really arrested the murderous rascal."

She stared big eyed at him, asking, "Are you suggesting my uncle and his deputies arrested an innocent man, Custis?"

To which he replied with a laugh, "Not hardly. Men picked up for no good reason tend to yell a lot for a lawyer and a writ of habeas corpus. The cuss your uncle wired us about fit the description of a known outlaw, and innocent saddle tramps just don't bust out of jail leaving that many dead lawmen in their wake. Old Dave Rice had good cause to suspect the stranger in town was up to no good. But I have discovered to my own disgust that lawyers won't let you hold a suspect on the grounds that you know it, in your bones, that he's up to something."

She looked relieved and said, "Oh, you're suggesting that poor Dave Rice planted that suspicious running iron in Sweet William's saddlebag as a good excuse to run him in, right?"

Longarm shrugged and said, "I can't see even an owlhoot as wild as Sweet William is supposed to be planting incriminating evidence on his fool self! I wish it wasn't so late for social calling. The next time I meet up with your uncle I mean to ask him, man to man with no pesky law clerk taking notes, how come they really ran Sweet William in. Meanwhile, they can't hardly hold anyone or anything up right now. So what say I help you with the dishes, ma'am?"

She dimpled at him, told him the dishes could stay overnight in the sink with no great harm to 'em, and added, "If I'm to call you Custis, you're going to have to call me Reggie, the way all my real friends do. Shall we go into the parlor now, or would you rather I show you to bed, upstairs?"

He wasn't sure how he ought to take that. There wasn't enough lamplight shining in her big blue eyes to read her smoke signals one way or the other. So he told her it was her house and left it up to her. She allowed that in that case they might as well get on up the stairs, it being so late and all.

As he followed her up he was pleasantly surprised by how well she knew how to signal with her shapely der-

33

riere. It likely had something to do with her having such a poetic nature. She didn't wiggle-waggle like a dance-hall gal or flirtatious squaw. She simply moved more side to side, albeit gracefully, than anyone really needed to just to mount a flight of steps, for Pete's sake.

It was dark at the head of the stairs. She told him to watch his step as she led him along a dimly moonlit landing to a door she unlocked with a key he hadn't noticed her carrying. It was even darker inside. As he stepped in after her she turned out to be somewhere less expected and he had to grab hold of her to keep them both from falling when they bumped so soft as well as firmly. He told her he was sure sorry and she told him, in a suddenly husky tone, that she didn't mind at all. Then they both laughed, awkwardly, and he had to let her go, even though he didn't really want to.

She struck a match and lit a penny candle atop the bitty table by the head of a big brass bedstead. By its measly glow he could see the room was female frilly as well as clean kept and smelling of lavendered linen. As she bent to pull the counterpane down from the plumped-up pillows with freshly ironed pillowcases, he felt obliged to compliment her on the immaculate condi-tion of the cozy bedroom, saying, "You sure keep your spare rooms tidy, considering you said you don't hire out spare rooms no more, Reggie."

She straightened up and turned to face him as she told him, sober faced but big eyed, "This isn't a guest room, Custis. It's mine."

So he thought it only natural to haul her in for some spit-swapping with one hand while he snuffed the can-dle with the other. As their lips and more met in the resulting dark, Regina Morpeth kissed back in a manner suggesting she wrote mighty sentimental poetry indeed. But when he eased her down across the mattress to go

34

roaming over her calico-covered curves with his free hand she demanded, "Whatever are you *doing*, Custis? Do big-city folk down in Denver respond like this to an innocent nighty-night kiss?"

He kissed her some more and got his hand up under her skirt a ways before he saw fit to defend his actions with mention of just where they were and who'd invited him there of her own free will. She gasped, "Oh, dear, I see how I might have given you the wrong impression! I only meant you could use this room, tonight, because I could see you'd had a long day and this bed was already made up. I naturally meant to put linens on another bedstead, just down the hall, and— Custis! Stop that this instant! What kind of a girl do you think I am?"

It would have been impolite to tell her she seemed sort of horny as well as experienced, judging from how wet she was where it counted, and how she was moving her hips in time with his gentle caresses. So he just kissed her some more, warmed her up some more, and gently allowed he'd stop if she just couldn't stand no more. She didn't answer with words, lest it turn out he really meant such foolish remarks, and so they were going at it hot and heavy when she finally begged him to stop teasing her and do it to her right, in just his socks with a pillow under her own sweet bare behind. But later, when he got a cheroot to share with her as they groped for their second winds, she told him he sure did it swell for such an unromantic and plainspoken cuss. She asked him how on earth he'd gotten her out of her dress and behaving so shameless, as she put it, without saying half the things Romeo had ever said to Juliet.

He lit his smoke, enjoying a drag, and let her suck on it as he assured her, "Romeo was Italian, and just a young squirt besides. I used to be a young squirt. But by the time I was shaving more regular than Romeo could have, I'd found out gals were more likely to bust out laughing than they were to let you kiss 'em, if you assured 'em of undying passion for their toenails and a mad desire to kiss them on both eyeballs."

She laughed despite herself and confided, "That sounds more painful than romantic. Maybe it's just as well as you don't croon and swoon like Romeo, at least where the neighbors might notice. We have to think of my reputation, now that you've had your way with me. For I fear I've already acquired one for being sort of, well, you know, bohemian, what with my writing poetry and all."

He suspected anyone who moved so fine in bed had been there before, more than once, with others the neighbors might or might not have noticed. But since that made her no worse than his own frisky self, he assured her he'd slip out some time between cockcrow and sunrise if she had an alarm clock to set for him. She said she did but demanded, in a somewhat injured tone, "Does that mean you have to go back to Denver at once, dear?"

He replied truthfully, "I won't know for certain until I get my instructions from Marshal Vail. He'll likely tell me to come on home and start the search from there."

She protested, "Sweet William never escaped from the Denver lockup, Custis!"

To which he replied with a wry chuckle, "He'd have had a time busting out of the Federal House of Detention we got there, even though such things have been known to happen. The point is that no matter where a crook lights out from, you've either got to trail him tight all the way or just wait for him to show up again somewhere else."

He took his smoke back. As he puffed it she pointed out, "You just said they could still be here in Arnold

36

Wells, fixing to rob the bank or Lord knows what-all, honey-lover!"

So he stuck the smoke back between her lips to point out, "They could just as easily be fixing to rob a bank or stop a train clean over the horizon in any direction, Reggie. I only said they *could* have sought shelter with some local householder. I never said I or anyone else could be sure, until such time as they come out from wherever they're hiding. I'll naturally warn the boys here in Arnold Wells to keep an eye on the one bank and anything else worth an outlaw's time and trouble. But to tell the truth I'll be mighty surprised if they hit anywhere in this stretch of Colorado, now that they've stirred things up so serious."

She set the cheroot aside and began to fondle a more inspiring cylindrical source of pleasure as she sort of pleaded, "Don't you think it's possible Sweet William and his friends might just want to lay low, here in town, indefinitely?"

He put one of his own hands on her wrist to help her move her hand a mite faster as he said, just as conversationally, "Crooks who don't do anything crooked are almost impossible to catch. We've been told Frank and Jesse are holed up respectable this summer, somewhere off their old stamping grounds in and about Clay County, Missouri. But leopards hardly ever change their spots and sooner or later the wayward rascals will just have to show up somewhere, dead or alive."

By now she had it almost up enough for both of them to enjoy. So he wedged a pillow where it would do them both the most good and rolled her aboard it as he added, "Sweet William Allan has yet to rob half as much money as the James and Younger boys. So he won't be able to hide out half as long on his ill-gotten gains. But you have my word as a gentleman-admirer that I'll be

37

proud to come this way if those rascals show up here in Arnold Wells again."

She wrapped her bare legs around his nude torso and hissed that she loved coming this way, as well. But he'd no sooner brought her to climax again and rolled her over to do it some more, than she commenced to sob and cuss as if he was hurting her instead of pleasuring them both. So he paused in midstroke to ask what was wrong and she bawled that it wasn't fair of him to expect her to get all she needed out of him in only one night. He laughed, not unkindly, and told her he'd been wondering why they'd had such strong black coffee just before bedtime, if sleeping was what she'd had in mind for either of them. But even as she called him an unfeeling brute she arched her spine to see how much more they both could feel.

Chapter 3

Nosy neighbors or not, Longarm didn't get out of there before nine A.M., and Regina Morpeth had to agree it was her own fault for neglecting to set that alarm. He suspected, slicking her so swell with soap while they enjoyed a hot bath together in tepid water, that she hadn't been all that worried about her reputation, considering the artistic way she finally waved him off, wearing nothing but that open kimono as he had to go down her front steps in broad daylight, trying not to walk funny or notice lace curtains moving in other windows all about.

He found Pop Purvis open for business again at the now much neater lockup. When he mentioned the bank within pistol range of the one front door, Pop allowed the thought had occurred to him and, pointing at the nearby gun rack, Pop added, "I've deputized my nephew, Freddy, and promoted some of the other boys I had part-time to full-time. I figure the only thing we really have to worry about would involve a few strange ponies tethered close enough and saddled serious enough to matter. There just ain't no other place to buy a meal or hire a bed less than a full day's ride from here. So they'd have to have bedrolls, at least, tied to their saddles, right?"

There were a few holes in that notion, but Longarm had a train to catch, and the older lawman was at least keeping one eye open. So he contented himself with, "I'd be more concerned with them having some local confederates hiding them, if they're anywhere around here at all, Pop. Young Fred pointed out and I agree that there just ain't that much deep woods and unexplored caverns amid all this light construction and wide-open shortgrass range."

Purvis nodded but sounded unconvinced as he objected, "Nobody here in Arnold Wells would hide such skunks for love or money, Longarm. I know everyone in town, personal, and while I can't say every one of 'em knows how to square the circle or spell Constantinople, we don't have any village idiot. Not idiotic enough to risk helping the cold-blooded killers of two popular local boys, at any rate. For between you and me, anyone caught acting so low down would as likely wind up high on a telegraph pole as on the gallows over to the county seat, if you take my meaning."

Longarm said he knew how small, tightly knit communities took care of real shits, and they parted friendly. He caught the southbound to Denver less than twenty minutes later and barely had time to finish a couple of beers and a copy of *Lesley's Illustrated Weekly* in the club car before it was time to get off again.

He had lunch at the Parthenon near the Federal Building, the Parthenon serving as fine a free lunch as

40

any saloon in Denver, and then it was back to the office, feeling stronger after stowing away some boiled eggs and picked pigs' feet after that sissy breakfast old Regina had cooked for him, bare-ass.

Henry, the prissy but sometimes tough young clerk who played the typewriter out front, looked surprised to see Longarm. He allowed their boss was in but said, "We figured you'd be on your way by now."

Henry was always making obscure remarks like that. He seemed to think he had a dry sense of humor. Longarm had told Henry, more than once, he was only required to laugh when someone said something that was really funny. Just plain silly didn't count. So he grumped past Henry and his machine to enter the oak-paneled inner office of his nibs, the original as well as fat and balding U.S. Marshal William Vail.

As Longarm strode over to the one big leather guest chair and sank down with an innocent yawn, the stubby Vail, seated behind the desk in his shirtsleeves and smoking a cigar that reminded Longarm of a dog turd, lit or not, scowled across the gulf of age and rank between them to demand, "What are you doing here, damn your eyes? Didn't you get the wire we sent you care of Western Union, Arnold Wells?"

Longarm reached for a smoke of his own as he nodded and said, "Sure I did, Billy. Your answer to my night letter was waiting for me there this morning. Unless I need specs worse than I thought, you wired me to come on back and leave the cold trail to the Indians."

As Longarm lit a cheroot Vail shook his bullet head and growled, "That was when we first opened up this morning, before we got the all-points from Gilpin County, around nine-thirty. Read it and weep all you like, but tell me first what you're doing here in Denver at a time like this, you lazy young rascal!"

Suiting actions to his words Billy Vail threw a balled up telegram at Longarm, who caught it one-handed and spread it to read. But before he could his impatient superior told him, "Sweet William and his henna-headed doxie passed through there once before, the time they stopped the mail stage, so they were recognized by a survivor of that particular federal offense when they got off the narrow gauge in the wee small hours. The damn fool ran direct to the town law without thinking to follow 'em to their destination in town."

Longarm had caught up with the tale on paper and consulted his memorized railroad timetables as well by this time, so he headed his boss off with, "They made damned good time if they were spotted there at five A.M. We're talking about twelve hours after Sweet William busted out of jail at Arnold Wells." Longarm grimaced and added, "The gal pulled a simple but slick misdirection on us. She told others up at Arnold Wells she needed two furnished rooms, allowing she'd show up with two men, later. The mere fact that pretty women ain't supposed to come at men, solo, with man-sized guns indeed, threw us off as well."

Vail snapped, "You explained in your night letter about them two deputies getting blown away by a Le Mat."

But Longarm shook his head and snapped back, "Two Le Mats. One in each dainty hand. Both lawmen got hosed down with pistol rounds and number-nine buckshot. One Le Mat fires nine rounds of .40 caliber and one freaky French shotgun shell. Add it up."

Billy Vail did, made a wry face, and said, "It ain't no secret that the female of the species can be more deadly than the male. They do say she's a looker, and even an ugly gal might find it easier to get the drop on two young bachelor lawmen. Get on to what that extra man they didn't really need might have had to do with 'em

42

making such saps outa you and the others hunting for 'em all over Arnold Wells last night."

Longarm smiled sheepishly and admitted, "I never spent the entire night hunting Sweet William and his Barbara Allan. I figured they were laying low with somebody local if they hadn't slipped out of town entire by, say, midnight."

He blew a thoughtful smoke ring and stared through it at the banjo clock on one oak-paneled wall, adding, "To make it so far before dawn they couldn't have tarried all that long in Arnold Wells. So I owe everyone up yonder an apology or a boot in the ass, depending."

Vail asked what depended on what, so Longarm elaborated, "Neither me nor Pop Purvis, the town law up yonder, could be everywhere at once. So we were forced to take some things on faith. Nobody in town saw two men leaving town with one woman, so they paid no attention to *one* man likely strolling arm-in-arm with a sweet little thing. You show me a community of even hard-shell Baptists that don't have any courting couples strolling about in the cool shades of evening and I'll show you a congregation on the road to extinction!"

Vail sighed and said, "They likely boarded any southbound coming through after dark, say from the far side of the tracks with the train between them and— Hold on, ain't Arnold Wells a *flag stop*?"

Longarm was back on his feet again as he replied, "It is, but how they got on up north is less important than where they got off this morning. I'll make it this side of sunset if I start right now!"

As he did so, Billy Vail followed him out to the front office. Neither of them were surprised by Henry having Longarm's travel orders and arrest warrants already typed up. Henry was supposed to tend to chores like that. As Longarm put his papers away under his frock

43

coat he told Henry, and Billy Vail if he was listening, "I'd like more poop on Sweet William Allan waiting for me here if I come back without him again. It's a pain in the ass to track down crooks you ain't sure about on sight, even when they don't have some slick tricks they use to keep you from sighting time to begin with!"

Henry rose from behind his desk, sidled over to a filing cabinet, and hauled out a manila folder, saying, "You can take along this dossier I've put together on the sneaky rascal, if you think it will do any good." But even as Longarm took it, Billy Vail grumbled, "Just *get* the son of a bitch. We aim to hang him, not write a book about him!"

Chapter 4

Central City, the seat of Gilpin County, was a little over thirty miles west-northwest of Denver by crow and somewhat farther by wagon trace or narrow gauge railroad. Springing as it had from the raw-pine gold sluice of old Johnny Gregory in a side canyon of Clear Creek, the town now consisted of tents, shacks, and more substantial attempts at carpentry erected hodge-podge wherever the ground seemed halfway level enough. If a wall canted oddly or a balloon frame rose sort of twisty hither and yon, nobody worried unless and until drinks slid off bars and whores fell out of bed.

Neither happened often, lately, since most of the early mine shafts close to town had already caved in by now. Central City still hauled its own high grade from the nearby Glory Hole, the first big open-pit operation of the American West, but as it approached its twentieth birthday Central City was commencing to serve more sedately as the financial and transportation center for surrounding and still brawling camps at Black Hawk, Tin Cup, French Gulch and such. Hence the indignation and frantic plea for federal assistance when a known associate of Jesse James had been spotted within the not-too-defined city limits of Central City.

As Longarm got off the narrow gauge late the streets of the dinky mountain town were shadowed purple as well as mighty steep in spots. For although the sky above was still a bright cloudless cobalt, the granite cliffs rising almost sheer all around lopped hours off the sunny parts of the day. Longarm knew it would stay about as light, albeit gloomy, for a spell. He still toted his personal saddle, carbine, and other possibles across the cinderpaved street to the Blossom Rock Hotel and hired himself a room before doing anything else. Once he'd assured himself by daylight that the sheets weren't speckled with bedbug shit and that the door lock seemed stout enough to guard his old McClellan and Winchester against casual mischief, he pocketed the key and mosied on up the slope to the county courthouse to pay a courtesy call on the local sheriff, whether the cuss knew where Sweet William might be now or not.

Sheriff Hiram Blake kept the peace in Gilpin County as best he could from an office that was either in the cellar or on the first floor of the courthouse, depending on which way one approached it. Blake was around the same age but better dressed and beefier than old Pop Purvis up where Sweet William Allan had last been picked up by the law. Sheriff Blake assured Longarm they were working on that down this way as he sat his guest, offered him a cigar, and sat back down to light one of his own when Longarm allowed he'd stick with his own cheroots for now. As they blew tobacco smoke back and forth at one another, Blake didn't add all that

46

much to what Longarm already knew. He cheerfully admitted he wouldn't know Sweet William or that dangerous redhead he was supposed to be running so wild with if he woke up in bed with them. Longarm didn't ask which the older lawman might kiss first. He said, "I left the folder we have on Sweet William at my hotel. I hope you'll take my word when I tell you that there was nothing about him riding with a henna-rinsed or any other sort of female in his freshman days with Frank and Jesse, farther east."

Sheriff Blake leaned back in his chair expansively to reply in a world-weary way, "Everything seems to wind up wilder out this way. That may be why they call it the Wild West. I know a lot of the stuff Ned Buntline whips up for his penny-dreadful magazines is pure bull, but you gotta admit we grow wilder women out this way than you meet in sissy places like Missouri."

Longarm made a wry face and replied, "I've bought a few drinks for Calamity Jane and vice versa. I've yet to decide whether she or Belle Starr would be more unsettling to kiss. But suffice it to say neither of them tough old gals have yet been known to bust into a town lockup, firing a Le Mat with both dainty fists."

Sheriff Blake nodded and said, "That redhead does sound like a real caution. But get to the point, old son. We both know somebody got Sweet William out of jail at Arnold Wells, and I once chased Mountain Charlie Forest through the mountains, not all that far from here. You heard about her, of course?"

Longarm nodded soberly and declared, "A mite before I started riding for Billy Vail and Uncle Sam, but I recall the legend."

Blake looked injured and said, "Bite your sassy young tongue! Mountain Charlie Forest was no legend. She was a real live and not bad looking gal of flesh and blood, even though she did pass herself off as a man in floppy shirts and baggy pants at times."

Longarm didn't want to talk about gunslicks, male or female, he hadn't been sent out after. So he nodded firmly and insisted, "I said I knew the story, legendary or, hell, true. Charlene Forest was the young widow of a mining man murdered, she said, by claim jumpers. They told another tale entire, of course, so when she couldn't get any satisfaction from the law she went after 'em personal, dressed up in men's duds to pass for a young boy with an old buffalo gun."

Sheriff Blake nodded in a nostalgic way and replied, "At least two of the poor souls she bushwhacked had to have been innocent. It was a great relief when she fell in love with a barkeep and gave up avenging her mining man."

Longarm said, "I can imagine what a load it took off everyone's mind. But I never said it was impossible for a woman to take up the shooting of mankind for fun and profit. I've arrested more than one member of the unfair sex for murder in my six or eight years with the Justice Department. I only said it was unusual, and that Sweet William's yellow sheets fail to list a homicidal female among his known associates in the Missouri hill country. Unless we assume he corrupted some innocent country gal considerable as well as recent, the two-gun redhead he took up with out our way ought to have some yellow sheets of her own in some damned file, see?"

Sheriff Blake did, but said, "The most dangerous female in our files goes by the handle of Battle Alice, a temperance advocate noted for busting up saloons with a fireman's axe, not a Le Mat pistol. Her hair is more mouse gray than red, by the way. Your best bet here in Central City would be old Grat Mooney, the cuss who

48

tipped us off about Allan and his doxie coming back to these parts. Mooney was a passenger aboard the mail stage from Winter Park the time they stopped it so cruel, last fall. As you likely know, there's no railroad over the Divide to Winter Park, so they send considerable mail and a heap of gold dust out by stagecoach."

Longarm nodded impatiently and said, "We have all the gory details on the warrants sworn out on the road agents who blew both the driver and shotgun messenger away for less than five hundred dollars total profit. I'm more interested in nailing Allan and that two-gun bitch he runs with before they kill anyone else. So how do I go about having me a serious talk with this Grat Mooney?"

The older lawman shot a glance at a wall clock that could have been a litter mate to Billy Vail's back in Denver, albeit nailed to whitewashed pine instead of varnished oak, and decided, "Bad time to look for anyone here in Central City, Longarm. It's pushing suppertime, with the work shifts up and down the canyon fixing to change. Old Grat works at the stamping mills above the smelter Senator Hill built us. Of course he thunk up the smelter before we elected him our senator in sheer gratitude, but—"

"Never mind where Mooney works if he's about to get off work," Longarm cut in. "Just tell me where in tarnation I can find him, some damned time this evening!"

Sheriff Blake nodded, hauled a notebook out of a desk drawer, and copied down a street address for Longarm on a little slip of foolscap.

Longarm scanned it, folded it, and tucked it away in a vest pocket. The sheriff walked him out front and, since he asked if there was anything else he could do, Longarm said he hadn't had his own supper yet and

49

asked where the nearest nonlethal eatery was that a deputy of his pay grade could afford. Old Hiram pointed at the lights just winking on farther along the canyon and confided, "Holy Moses, across from Star-Spangled Supplies, will feed you about the most for the least if your gut can abide Chinese cooking." So Longarm allowed he admired chop suey almost as much as chili con carne and they shook on that and parted friendly.

In the tricky light even deeper in the slot the skinny stringbean of a town occupied he'd have had a time finding the Oriental joint without the assistance of Star-Spangled Supplies, selling anything from dynamite caps to hoist machinery and bragging about it in big red letters across a false front painted baby blue and spattered with badly drawn six-pointed stars. Not craving dynamite caps or even dynamite for supper, Longarm squinted across the narrow rutted way for guidance until he made out a modest sign with HONG LEE MAO inscribed under some Chinese lettering that made even less sense to Longarm. He felt more certain he was on the right track when he approached the dim-lit doorway and sniffed the tempting odors of down-home cooking, if your home happened to be Canton or Shanghai. Blake had neglected to tell him the place was a walk-up. But right now he felt hungry enough to climb all the way out of the fool canyon. So he went on up the narrow stairs in the tricky light until he found himself on a landing, facing a plank door painted the color of fresh-spilt blood with nothing in the way of a knob. It struck him as an odd way to attract customers but apparently they expected you to knock. So he was about to when he heard mighty unfriendly noises on the far side and held his fire to cock one ear to the crimson planking.

The muffled female voice on the far side was protesting in Chinese, or Greek, for all Longarm could make of it. But there was no mistaking the urgency of her tone or the evil intent of the male voice warning her in plain American to shut up and take what he had for her as the great honor intended. So Longarm muttered, "Damn it, I was only looking to enjoy a quiet meal!" as he backed off as far as the landing would let him and then hit the door hard as he could with his left shoulder.

The door burst inward, its latch never having been intended to stop anything the size of Longarm with a full head of steam. As he'd thrown his full weight against the crimson planking he'd as naturally drawn his .44-40 with his right hand. So as the big galoot inside rolled off the Chinese lady he'd been trying to rape atop a sort of writing desk, Longarm pistolwhipped him even farther off her before he could get his own side arm, a .45 Walker Conversion, clear of its own holster.

The lusty lad of, say, forty was tough as he looked, for even after he'd wound up in a far corner of the tiny room with a lot of blood and at least one tooth dribbling down his unshaven chin he said mean things about Longarm's mother and kept trying to haul his fool gun out. Longarm booted him in the head before he could figure out he was sitting on the other end of the holster with most of his big ass. The kick, or the way it banged his head against the wall behind him, inspired him to just flop over on top of his six-gun in sweet repose. So Longarm turned to the Chinese lady, ticked his hat brim to her, and said, "Evening, ma'am. I was looking for a chop suey parlor and this looks more like someone's office."

She answered him, or spoke to him at any rate, in her own singsong tongue as she stood by the desk, smoothing down her sheath dress of black silk brocade. At second glance she was no spring chicken. For there were silver threads among the black bangs above her almond eyes. But she was still a pretty gal and built well besides. So there was no great mystery as to what that roughly dressed white man reposing in the corner had been after. He said, "Well, no real harm done, and I reckon I can drag him down the stairs for you, ma'am."

Then her eyes widened and she shouted louder than ever in Chinese. So as Longarm spun about to see what she'd been staring at with such concern, behind him, the big Chinaman wearing a white apron and holding a big meat cleaver ominously high stared just as puzzled at Longarm while the Chinese lady jabbered at him some more. Longarm couldn't savvy word-one, but he was able to follow her drift when the younger but way heavier set Oriental commenced to lower his impressive kitchen cutlery and favor Longarm with a big toothy smile. Then he said, in fair English, "Our house is in your debt, American sir. How shall you be called, in order that our great great grandchildren may properly honor your great great grandchildren in the centuries to come?"

Longarm said, "Aw, mush. I'm U.S. Deputy Custis Long and it's my duty to do what I just now had to do. Lucky for this lady, here, I was looking for your restaurant, wherever it may be, and stumbled up to this office or whatever just in time. I'd best just drag this polecat up to the town lockup for you and—"

"We'll take care of him," the big Chinese man cut in with an ominous nod at the unconscious brute in the corner. "You come downstairs and let us feed you like a mandarin, eh? More better you let us clean up own mess with protection boys."

Longarm cocked an eyebrow, turned to regard the knocked-out tough with the distaste inspired by full understanding, and shook his head to say, "I follow your drift. I can't argue with the rough justice of your own informal solution. But like I just told you, I'm a law-man. So we'd best deal with this uncouth rascal constitutional. I'm on pretty good terms with your Sheriff Blake. So I'll just run this cuss upslope as soon as he can stand on his own two feet and——"

"More better we just forget all about it!" the China-man cut in with a worried aside in Cantonese to his mother, aunt, or whatever. She looked downright sick as she singsonged back in the same lingo.

So Longarm said, "You folk may have a time buying this, but you can tell me if your local law is in cahoots with ruffians shaking you folk down. I know the memories of the so-called Chinese Riots must be fresher to you than the rest of us, but they were never approved by the federal government and everyone but maybe pure-blood Indians do have certain rights us federal deputies are obliged to back up."

The big Oriental sighed and said, "This is Gilpin County, not an army post or Indian reserve. We have to live here after you have to leave. Down in Leadville they don't allow us or any other colored people to live at all. Things have not been so bad up this way. Why can't we just forget it?"

The brute in the corner was commencing to stir and mutter some. Longarm moved over, hunkered down to roll the cuss off his six-gun and disarm him before he slapped some life into the foiled rapist, saying, "Rise and shine, Sleeping Beauty. This seems to be your lucky night. These folk don't want to press charges after all. So what say we head you on back to your snake pit and let 'em run their business right some more?"

"I'll get you for this," the battered bully growled in a groggy way as Longarm hauled him to his feet.

Longarm smiled fondly and told him, "Not here. Are you up to walking down them stairs outside or would you rather I flung you down 'em? I ain't about to carry a bundle of trash your size, so what's it going to be?"

The man he'd pistolwhipped and kicked into a state of domesticated helplessness allowed he could get down the stairs if only Longarm would hang on to him a mite. So with the big Chinaman following them, Longarm got the muttering cuss down to the dirt street. There, he told the Oriental he might be back for some fresh fried rice, hundred-year-old eggs, or whatever they were serving, as soon as he saw this other devotee of Far Eastern pleasures up the canyon a piece. The young chef with the meat cleaver told him they'd treat him right when he got back. So Longarm frog-marched the would-be rapist up the street to a dark stretch, swung him into a slot between two buildings, and slammed him against a board-and-baton wall to inform him, sternly, "I'd hit you some more if I wasn't worried about you puking on my boots. For I somehow doubt you've fully grasped the advantages of leaving Chinese women the hell alone. They're scarce as hens' teeth and more valued than rubies by their menfolk on this side of the Pacific pond. So had I left you to your own devices back there you'd have no doubt wound up dead, or wishing you were. I get along pretty good with decent folk of any description, but I have to admit some gents from old Cathay display a mighty mean streak when you get 'em really riled at you."

The big brute was beginning to recover, it seemed, for he managed a coarse laugh and muttered, "Thanks for nothing but a couple of busted teeth, you durned old Chink lover. I knew what I was doing. They need to be reminded when they're slow with their payments. I wasn't fixing to really hurt the Widow Lee. A good fuck and maybe a few bruises would have straightened her out, right?"

Longarm shook him the way a terrier shakes a rat, saying, "Wrong. I'm telling you, not asking you, to leave those folk alone. Lucky for you, my boss don't allow me to bring in petty pests who steal pennies off dead folk's eyelids or shake down shoestring businesses for petty cash. So if you make me come at you again it'll be personal and informal, if you follow my drift."

The thug was really beginning to feel better now. He drew himself to full height and sneered, "You ain't the law in this here town. So who are you to threaten me with what?"

Longarm kneed him in the balls and punched the howling results with a rawboned uppercut that put the poor dumb brute out of its misery some more. Then he took a leak, aiming neither at nor away from the pile of trash at his feet, and went back to Hong Lee Mao's again.

This time he found the right entrance on the ground floor. It was just about as dark inside, and someone had gotten a buy on that blood-red paint. As he hung up his hat and sat himself down in a corner booth, a young Chinese gal dressed more American than the older one upstairs came out through a beaded curtain to kiss him on the cheek and say, "Trust cousin Fang in kitchen. You wouldn't know how to order really fine meal you deserve for what you do on boss lady."

He smiled up at her and replied, "It wasn't me out to do anything on her, miss. As for what I'd like for supper, I sure like the way you folk fry rice and—"

"No fried rice! No egg roll! No chop suey!" she cut in. "Cousin Fang gonna feed you like *guest*, not like customer!"

So he laughed, relaxed, and enjoyed it as the pretty little thing brought him serving after serving of stuff he couldn't pronounce, even after she'd told him what he was eating. He ate so much, partly to keep from hurting their feelings and partly because it all tasted so swell, that he was sure he'd never want to eat again for a month. The only thing he didn't think much of was a sort of bland custard she introduced him to as a luxury dessert only rich folk could afford back home in Canton. He managed to get about a quarter of it down. But it was just as well, he thought, he wasn't a rich old Chinaman if this was all they got out of it at suppertime.

He already knew better than to put cream or sugar in the tea or ask how come Chinese teacups had no handles. As she poured him yet another cup, the pretty little gal confided, "We talking on you out back since you beat on that Bummer. You not safe from Bummers if you sleeping in hotel they protecting!"

He sipped some tea to sort all that out before he told her, "If you're saying the gang that's been shaking down fold up here in the high country are in any way related to the infamous Denver Bummers, I've always wondered where they ran off to after the Colorado Militia cracked down on 'em a few years back. As to whether the Blossom Rock Hotel may be managed by friends or foes of such roughnecks, I'll cross that bridge when I get to it. Right now I have to look up a witness to more serious skulduggery."

He got out the name and address of old Grat Mooney and showed it to the pretty waitress. She told him, "Rough neighborhood across gulch. No Chinaboy go so close, hard-luck shanty town, oh my. Bad place in broad daylight. You big fool to go now with Bummer gang maybe look to get back on you!"

He sighed and said, "You'd be surprised at some of the dark and sinister neighborhoods my job requires me to visit, miss. I know *I've* never gotten used to it. But the taxpayers of these United States expect an honest

56

return on the five hundred dollars and change a year they pay me to maintain law and order. So I'd best get cracking, and what do I owe you for all this swell grub?"

She told him not to be silly and to keep her and her kith and kin in mind the next time he needed food, shelter, or anything else he might want in Central City. Only, when he asked, she couldn't tell him beans about Sweet William or his murderous Barbara Allan. So he put on his hat to go looking for someone who might.

Chapter 5

Grat Mooney seemed to be one of those natural talkers who enjoyed a good gab, drunk or sober. Once they'd worked out who Longarm might be and what he was doing so far upslope so late at night, the old-timer hauled him inside the one-room shanty, sat him down at the packing crate he'd turned into a table, and poured them both heroic tumblers of Magnolia brand whiskey. As Mooney sat himself down across from his younger guest, Longarm felt it safe to assume the old cuss had poured himself a few earlier ones since getting off work at the stamping mill. Magnolia was so called because it was supposed to be fine old Southern bourbon. In point of fact it was likely safer to drink than paint remover, after which little more could be said for it. But the old machinist made enough sense to follow, if one allowed for a few slurred words and repetitions here and there. He said he'd first met up with the deadly duo the previous fall, as the sheriff had already said, while riding over James Pass as the only male passenger aboard the mail stage. He said the female passenger seated across from him had been the sort of hard-eyed lady known as Barbara Allan, albeit he hadn't known this right off and allowed he'd tried to talk to her, without much luck, until they'd suddenly been stopped in a draw and ordered to get out with their hands full of sky.

He sighed and said, "Neither me nor the stage crew figured the young gal as armed and dangerous, of course. I confess I was worried about her honor, more fool me, as I helped her down to the roadway and warned her to do as the road agent said and offer him neither resistance nor unexpected moves."

Longarm soberly suggested, "You sound like a man who'd been held up more than once."

The old-timer replied with a wry look of resignation, "I been out here since the first color was found down in Cherry Creek. That's what we used to call Denver afore it got so fancy, Cherry Creek."

He poured himself more encouragement and continued, "That sassy gal with her fake red hair bound up with artificial silk ribbons likely knew lots more than me about holdups, though. For when it turned out we'd been stopped, we thought, by one lone road agent, the shotgun messenger must have recalled what he'd been hired for and bent over, sudden, for the scatter-gun he had down out of sight in the boot, with the strongbox and such."

Longarm nodded understandingly and said, "I heard things turned out bad for both him and the driver. It may be brave but it sure ain't smart to reach for a gun with another one covering you."

But Mooney said, "He might have made it. The jehu was reaching for his own gun at the same time, and that road agent had to consider me as well, even though I wasn't armed under my loose coat. The gal tipped the difference, whipping her own whore pistol outa nowhere to blow the poor shotgun messenger headfirst off his perch with a bullet up his ass or close to said tender spot. Her boyfriend blew the jehu outa the driver's seat with that cannon he was aiming and that's about all I noticed, since I'd lit out downhill through the junipers lest they serve me the same way!"

Longarm told him, "You likely saved your own life by moving so unexpected. The pair seems anxious to avoid leaving witnesses alive in their bloody wake. But back up and go over the way they were armed again, pard."

Mooney thought, drunk as he might or might not have been, and insisted, "The young gent, Sweet William, was armed with this big old revolver gun, a Lee something, the sheriff's department decided when I described it to 'em later. The gal had been hiding a bitty .32 nickel-plated double-action all the time. It may have been a Harrington-Richardson. I know it was double-action 'cause she fired it fast and a lot, considering how often she could hit anything."

Longarm said, "You only have to hit one time if you put one in a poor boy's ass, unexpected. We had the gal down as armed with one or more infernal Le Mat machines. Of course, it stands to reason that she'd use any weapon handy, and her lover-boy was picked up in Arnold Wells armed more normal."

He scowled thoughtfully down at the amber contents of his own tumbler as he pondered some on such details and then asked Mooney, "You're certain the pair that stopped your stage, as well as the pair you reported seeing here more recent, have to be Sweet William and Barbara Allan?"

60

The old-timer shook his head and replied, "Nope. They could be *named* most anything as far as I could prove or, hell, hazard a guess. I never said I'd been introduced formal to that hard-eyed redhead and her lethal lover-boy, Longarm. I only said the pair I seen getting off the narrow gauge the other morning were the same pair as robbed the Winter Park stage and scared me outa a year's growth that time."

Longarm hadn't brought along the dossier Henry had prepared back in Denver for his use. But he was blessed, or cursed, with an almost photographic memory. So he said, "Let's go over 'em more nitpicky, Grat. William Allan, born in the County of Clay, Missouri, to kin of Zerelda James Samuel nee Cole, the dear sweet momma of Frank and Jesse James, describes as a slender-built jasper of medium height with curly brown hair and dark brows as meet in the middle and don't match the lighter locks atop his handsome head."

Old Grat grimaced and replied, "I didn't find him half as good-looking as the gal, and she acted really ugly. But, yep, I've been over the bushy eyebrows of the young cuss with you lawmen more than once. It's you gents, not me, who keep saying it has to be Sweet William Allan. I hope I never see him and that mean young gal again. I like to shit my pants when they walked past me at the depot without noticing me, I hope."

Longarm asked what the old-timer had been doing on the narrow gauge from Denver at that hour to be told, "Coming up from Denver, of course. I had to give a niece away at her wedding. I can't say what Sweet William and that other young gal might have been doing down yonder. I never saw 'em get on the train. I only saw 'em get off, when it stopped up here and almost made me shit my pants!"

Longarm asked if the old-timer had thought to follow the outlaw pair he'd recognized, only to be asked, "Do I look that drunk to you? Like I told the sheriff when he asked me the same dumb question, I lived through meeting up with those mean kids, twice. I wasn't about to tempt fate by tailing them two infernal feet! The moment I spotted 'em in the depot I ducked behind a platform pillar and stayed put there until I was sure everyone else had left. If you'd like an educated guess, they left by way of the front entrance. After that your guess is as good as mine. They ain't at any of the better hotels or boardinghouses in town. Sheriff Blake sent his deputies to look as soon as I told him who'd just come in by train with me."

Longarm didn't ask about less respectable hotels and rooming houses. He knew the sheriff and his boys would know more about such matters than an old machinist who didn't pack his own side arms. He took a polite sip of Magnolia brand, leaving some in the tumbler to discourage his host from pouring a refill, and said, "Well, they've passed through this stretch of the mountains before and must have hidden out somewhere in the county after they stopped that stage you were on. So the question before the house is not why they might have come back this way after that jailbreak but *where*. You say you recall Denver when it was still a rough little mining camp, before the war. I was told earlier this evening that some of the original Denver Bummers may have wound up here in Gilpin County after Marshal Tom Pollock tamed the new town a mite."

The old-timer refilled his own glass, raised it as if to toast at least Queen Victoria, and soberly said, "Here's to Noisy Tom Pollock, even if he was half bullshit. For I was there the night Marshal Pollock bearded the Bummers in their very den, the Criterian Saloon run by the dangerous Charley Harrison. The *Rocky Mountain News* dubbed the resultant confusion the Big Turkey War because it all began when the Bummers stole a wagonload of turkey birds off a poor old Mex called Picketwire. Marshal Pollock pistol-whipped a Bummer called McCarty and then—"

"Hold it. I just said Marshal Pollock cleared the Bummers out, with a little help from the state militia. The question before the house is how tied-in with that old criminal clan your Central City Bummers might be."

The old-timer grimaced and said, "I've heard about some of the riffraff up this way describing themselves as Bummers. Between you and me I think they're full of it. Whether you want to credit Sheriff Blake or the higher wages they pay up here these days, there just hasn't been all that much blood and slaughter up here, next to rougher camps like Leadville or Jimtown. You see, Noisy Tom Pollock shot it out with George Steele and arrested the ferocious Charley Harrison without no struggle. Them two and maybe old Carroll Woods was about as tough as the original Bummers came. Then we had the big war with the Southern states and a lot of rough old Denver boys got killed fighting on either side. It ain't tough in the gold fields like it used to be, Longarm. You should have been out here when the vigilance committee we called the Stranglers were dispensing justice, firm but fair. I mind the time they strung up Johnny Shear, Jake Ford, and Black Hawk for stealing ponies, back in the good old days."

Longarm said he'd been told he'd missed a heap of fun by coming west after misspending so much time in the War Between the States. Then he frowned and said, "Hold on. I thought Black Hawk was the name of another mining camp just east of here, Grat. Are you saying it's the handle of an early Colorado horse thief, associated with another crook named Ford?"

The old-timer nodded and said, "Black Hawk was a morose breed, if not a full-blood. Whatever he was, both the Ute and Araps had been convinced they'd live longer if not no better anywhere but the Rocky Mountain gold fields. So Black Hawk was living more white and stealing more white, with a white gang, when the Stranglers put an end to his career. What's a long-dead Indian horse thief got to do with that young couple you and Sheriff Blake are hunting in the here and now?"

Longarm decided he could use another drink, after all, as he said, "It could be no more than coincidence, but I reckon I'd best pay a serious visit to a mining camp named for a crook who died in the company of anyone named Ford. It's a common enough name for honest men as well as horse thieves, but Sweet William is said to be a known associate of the James boys, and so are Bob and Charley Ford!"

Heading back downhill toward the brighter lights along the bottom of the slot, Longarm should have been able to spot anyone between him and his hotel before they could spot him. So it raised the hairs on the nape of his neck and inspired his gun hand to streak across his gut and produce some hardware when he suddenly found himself striding down the steep path in step with a shadowy silent form.

The spooky outline pleaded, "Don't shoot, I'm with you!" in a voice tinged with just a hint of fried rice and soy sauce.

Since Longarm had the drop on the mysterious cuss, he contented himself for now with, "I've often wondered why you boys pad about in them felt-soled slippers. If you're on my side, how come you're acting so damned spooky?"

The Oriental replied, "You can't go back to the Blossom Rock Hotel. They have set up an ambush for you there. More better you come home with me, now."

Longarm frowned and decided, "I'm not even putting this gun away before I know you better. My saddle and all are at the hotel, and how do I know you're not trying to lead me into a trap instead of vice versa, stranger?"

His almost invisible would-be guide replied, "Your things have been removed from the hotel and stored in safer quarters by the same humble hotel help who spotted the other side moving into position."

"What other side?" asked Longarm.

"Think back no further than just before supper at Hong Lee Mao's and consider whose side you chose of your own free will, Deputy Long. You refused to let us deal with that wild animal as wild animals should be dealt with. You let it live. Creatures like that run in packs, after dark. The boss lady you saved from rape, robbery or worse told me to lead you to safer quarters. Please hold out your free hand. I wish to place the proof of my sincerity in it."

Longarm stepped sideways on the steep cinder path to hold his left hand out to the Oriental. The six-gun he was handed, grips first, had a .45 frame, whatever it fired, and one of those long-dong barrels Chinese hatchet men favored for some reason. He hefted the weapon thoughtfully and handed it back, saying, "I follow your drift. You'd be dumb as hell trying to lead me into an ambush with sweet talk after slipping up behind me with all this weaponry at your disposal. But look here, if you got a gun, and I got a gun, and you have other pals with guns, what's to stop us from just going on over to the Blossom Rock and turning any survivors over to the sheriff?"

His Oriental guide laughed bitterly and replied, "To

what purpose? Do you really think even an honest Colorado court could impanel a whole jury willing to convict other white men of anything on the word of a Chinaman?"

Longarm pointed out, "My eyes don't slant all that much, no offense."

But his would-be rescuer pointed out, "You don't have anything on anyone without our word to back you. I hope you won't be offended when I say you are not the only decent American who's ever been willing to stand up for simple justice, no matter how its eyes may slant. But trying to take the part of a despised minority against a majority that is at best indifferent—"

"I reckon I'd best get something on 'em more serious than mere attempted rape or murder," Longarm cut in. "I'm here on a more important case, or at least I thought I was. But as long as I'm here I'd best look into this other gang. You're gonna have to give me some names, dates and places, though. I can't shilly-shally with cases the local law's supposed to cope with. Matter of fact, I'm not supposed to stick my nose into non-federal cases at all. But what the hell, I don't see how even my stuffy boss can fault me for taking it personal when bush-league thugs come at me personal."

That settled, he listened intently as the Oriental led him through the bewildering maze of wildly canted shacks and filled him in on local law at the same time.

Hiram Blake, according even to folk he didn't see fit to help worth mention, seemed no worse than, if not a cut above, most Rocky Mountain lawmen when it came to protecting the rights of anyone neither Anglo-Saxon nor invited up to the gold fields to begin with. It was a tough enough chore protecting his own kind from claim jumpers, high-graders and other dangerous pests in an election year, where every arrest figured to cost a man a good many votes come November. Since heathen Chinese had no more call to vote than blacks, Arapaho, or womenfolk, Sheriff Blake discouraged the bullying and shaking down of Central City's few Chinese businessmen, but seldom pushed it past a stern warning or a gentle boot in the ass. There was no mystery as to the identity of the gang. There were only around a dozen. Neither the sheriff nor the white merchants they were careful not to victimize considered any of them really dangerous. When Longarm pointed out that ambushing a federal lawman near the center of town had to qualify as downright surly, his Oriental guide pointed out that they'd just deny it if he accused them, and that the only way he could prove it for certain would leave him in rotten shape to testify against anybody. So he muttered, "Since you put it that way, my best bet's a good night's sleep and an early start for Black Hawk, where things don't sound so complicated. I'm authorized to arrest Sweet William or his Barbara Allan on sight!"

The Oriental said his boss lady would no doubt want to provide him with a mount, come sunrise.

A short time later, although Longarm would have been stumped to find the place by daylight, they wound up in a sort of egg crate of stuck-together frame construction built to Chinese notions of house planning despite the Yankee two-by-fours and clapboard siding. His guide turned Longarm over to a pair of giggly young gals, who led him in turn to a small but lushly decorated room, filled mostly by a monstrous bed slung low on squatty gilt-wood legs and covered with crimson silk brocade. As one of the sweetly built young gals turned the covers down for him he decided the Widow Lee had to own at least one of the local gold mines along with her chop suey parlor. For while some Chinese could and did manage opium and fan-tan habits on the profits of laundries, eateries, and such, genuine Chinese *women* cost a hell of a lot to import since the railroad and mining unions had stirred up such a fuss about the U.S. being taken away from "real Americans" by thundering herds of Chinamen. Having learned in school about those sappy Indians teaching the pilgrims to plant corn, Longarm sometimes suspected some "real Americans" of suffering just a mite from a guilty conscience. But he got along all right with just about anyone who wasn't out to bust his head, or federal law. So he thanked the young ladies, and when one even slid a red panel aside to show him where they'd stored his saddle and other possibles, he blessed them as well and started to get undressed.

That was when he discovered they didn't go with the big fat bed, as he'd sort of hoped. As they giggled out on him he sat down with a sigh, grunted off his boots, and decided not to light a last cheroot after all when he saw there was nothing in the way of an ashtray and the infernal shag rug was too pale a shade of cream to hide tobacco ash. He threw all his duds on the rug instead and snuffed the one red candle by the bed before he rolled under the slithery silk covers. He fluffed up a pillow and tried lying on one side when the sensual silk started giving him a hard-on. He muttered, "Lord have mercy, even an ugly fat gal would feel grand beside one in a yummy bed like this one!"

But since there wasn't any female, fat and ugly or otherwise, he determined to get some shut-eye, knowing he faced a day no more restful than the one he'd just plodded through, cuss Sweet William and his restless ways.

Then he heard a mousy scrape, and the movement of air on his exposed bare shoulder told him someone had slid the door open in the dark. He slid his gun hand silently toward the bed table, where he'd left his pocket watch and derringer handy for just such events as these. But as he armed himself against his invisible visitor she rolled under the covers on the far side, purring at him like a big old pussy cat. So he ran his bare hands over her sandalwood-scented naked charms to make sure she packed no weapons of her own and, having made sure there was no place she could have hidden a hatpin, he pet her until he had her purring, serious. But as he kissed her shell-like ear and muttered sweet suggestions into it he learned she spoke little or no English. For he'd suggested they slide a pillow under her firm rump, and found it a mite confusing but not at all upsetting when she took the matter in hand and proceeded to stand it to full attention with tightly pursed lips and astoundingly twisty tongue. When he told her he wanted to finish right, atop her and that pillow, damn it, she got on top of him, instead. So he just gave up, leaned back and enjoyed it. As he played with her small firm breasts while she gyrated above him in the dark, he tried to picture which of the two chambermaids his downright gracious hostess had sent to make him feel so at home. He knew it couldn't be that English-speaking waitress, damn it, for she'd been mighty pretty. Of the two he'd just shared some bedtime giggles with, he'd noticed the one with the best shape had been sort of bucktoothed, while the really pretty little thing had been a mite flat chested under her silk sheath. He knew this one wasn't her. When he hauled her down against his bare chest to kiss her experimentally, her teeth felt about right and her lips, as he'd already noticed, puckered soft and lush. She seemed flattered by the notion of his wanting to kiss her at the same time. He was glad he'd made her feel so happy as she commenced to move her firm bottom up down and sideways in a way that threatened to leave

69

him in midair if he didn't exercise more control of the final charge. So he rolled her over on her back, without taking himself out of her, and although he'd thought she'd need a pillow under such a shapely but bitty behind, she didn't. For once she'd locked her naked calves around the nape of Longarm's neck she was able to come up to meet him in a series of ball-bouncing engulfments that would have been scary if he hadn't worked himself up about as hot. He doubted anyone could get quite as hot as this sandalwood-scented and now sort of musky tail-wagger. It made him like her and what he was doing to her even better. For even if she was only a servant ordered to service a guest, it seemed clear she was really enjoying the task. As he pounded her even harder he groaned, "I like you too, you little play-pretty, and I wish I knew how to say I was coming in your lingo. For I'd like to get you to come with me, if only I knew how."

But as it turned out, they managed that problem just swell, for whether by female intuition or the way she felt him moving in her at the last she suddenly flung her four limbs to the four corners of the darkness, and if she wasn't informing him in Cantonese that she was coming too, he failed to savvy what other wonders could be transpiring in her pulsating little love-maw as she tried to bite him off inside of her and might have, had she had any teeth at all down there.

After a lay like that it took Longarm a spell to catch his second wind. He started to grope for matches and a smoke, if only to catch a glimpse of the beauty he knew had to be there. Then he recalled the lack of any place to dump his ashes and decided, what the hell, there were some things a man was just as well off not studying on too hard.

In the dark, like this, he had her pictured pretty as

Helen of Troy could have been, and common sense told him nothing she had to show his eyes could be any improvement on the perfection his own naked flesh kept encountering in the cozy darkness. So he encountered her some more as soon as they could get it up for him again. She seemed a good sport about any position he could fondle her into and managed to come up with more than one he hadn't dared suggest, being more accustomed to ladies influenced by Queen Victoria's notions of proper fornication lest one wind up in a madhouse for the depraved.

So while he didn't remember her putting him to sleep with her purry lovemaking, he realized she had when he woke up, alone in bed, with a damned old canyon jay yelling it was morning. From where he lay in the dark atop rumpled bedding Longarm had to study some on that announcement. There was a chill in the darkness he hadn't felt before, and when he tried to go back to sleep he didn't feel sleepy. So he lit the candle and consulted his pocket watch to discover it was going on six, straight up!

Someone must have been watching the slit under the door for that candle flame. There came a discreet rap on the same, and when he said it was jake with him the door slid open to admit the same young gals with both his breakfast and bowl of warm washup water. One slid open a bitty window panel he hadn't known was there. Then they left him to his own wistful devices for a spell. The fresher but smelter-scented air from outside combined with the smell of his warm breakfast to erase the musky sandalwood fragrance of a night he surely meant to remember fondly. As he dressed he spied a couple of human hairs, straighter and stiffer than his own, on the pillow her sweet kissable head had dented next to his. He smiled softly and put them in a shirt pocket. By the

71

time he was fully dressed and had his old McClellan and Winchester out of that hidey-hole and over by the door, the male Chinese who'd led him down off the dark slope the night before came in to tell him they'd scouted around the hotel and that the Bummers had apparently given up for now.

Longarm gave his gun rig a hitch to ride his .44-40 handier as he growled, "I haven't given up on them. But first I got to ride over to Black Hawk. I seem to have a bigger apple to take care of than I figured on. I generally eat any apple one bite at a time. You did say something about loaning me a pony, didn't you?"

The Chinaman nodded and helped Longarm through the maze of hallways and courtyards with his gear until they found themselves in a stable facing out on the more American parts of Central City. As Longarm saddled and bridled the frisky buckskin barb, the Chinaman said it was his for as long as need be. The friendly Oriental gent added, "The Widow Lee gave orders we were to provide you with anything you have any use or desire for. She asked me to tell you she would have come down to see you off, herself, but that she feels shy about her English and knows you will understand."

Longarm nodded and said he sure did. He figured he'd get rid of those silvery hairs he'd found on that pillow after he'd ridden on a piece, lest he embarrass his sweet-screwing hostess further.

Chapter 6

The nearby camp of Black Hawk turned out to be named after the Black Hawk Mine rather than a lynched horse thief. But on reflection, the barkeep serving Long-arm needled beer and local history for the price of one allowed the mine could have been named after that thieving Indian of the prewar pioneer days. All the mining outfits in Gilpin County had been well established before the blue and the gray had gone to war, with a few attempts by Confederate raiders to finance their own side with western gold. As Longarm sipped on his side of the bar the barkeep wiped the mahogany between them with a damp rag, musing half to himself, "It wasn't my fight. So I had no call to mix in it on either side. But fair is fair and the first strikes in these here Rocky Mountains *were* made by *Southern* boys, you know."

Longarm shrugged and said, "The way they tell it

down at the Parthenon Saloon in Denver, the first prospector who ever came down out of these hills with color to show for panning a beaver stream was a Cherokee gent called Falling Leaf."

The barkeep shook his head and insisted, "Placer gold don't count. Any damn fool with a pan and nothing better to do can pan a few cents' worth of color a day out of most any creek west of the Big Muddy. It was Johnny Gregory, an otherwise worthless Georgia cracker, who first sunk pickax-one into the blossom rock. A lot of the other early birds hailed from the South as well."

Longarm didn't want to drink two beers in the same place so he set the schooner aside and lit a cheroot as he said, "Silver Dollar Tabor hailed from Vermont. But your point's well taken. I heard about 'em hoisting the Stars and Bars above Wallingford and Murphy's General Store in Denver right after they fired on Fort Sumpter, and we all know how General Sibley marched his Texas brigade as far north as Glorieta Pass, New Mexico Territory, and how the Rocky Mountain gold fields the North depended on for so much of its hard currency were saved by an otherwise useless son of a bitch called Butcher Chivington."

The barkeep brightened and said, "Oh, I've heard of Colonel Chivington and how he disgraced the Colorado Militia at Sand Creek, slaughtering the wrong tribe of Indians."

Longarm grimaced and said, "Would that real history kept its heroes and villains as neatly separate as Sir Walter Scott or even Ned Buntline. For I agree Chivington was a bloodthirsty shit at the so-called Battle of Sand Creek, but earlier, at the Battle of Glorieta Pass, he covered himself with glory no man can deny him. For Sibley was hammering his way north with over

74

three thousand Texas troops when Chivington circled to take him from the rear with no more than four hundred Colorado riders, burned eighty-odd Confederate supply wagons, ran off or butchered five hundred head of spare riding stock, and in sum discouraged any further Southern grabs at Northern gold fields. He did things right as a major. They promoted him to colonel for what he did at Glorieta Pass and had to bust and drum him out of the service in disgrace for what he did to the South Cheyenne at Sand Creek with a whole damned regiment at his disposal."

The barkeep put a head on Longarm's beer schooner, on the house without being asked, so Longarm knew he was stuck there until he could pay for at least another. He said, "I wasn't sent up here to refight dumb old wars, pard. I'm out to cut the trail of a young couple who couldn't have ridden for either side. But as I told you when I first came in to pester you, Sweet William Allan was supposed to have picked up some tips of the trade from rascals who did ride in the war, or at least they keep saying they did. Frank James may well have ridden with Quantrill, speaking of murderous shits. I take his kid brother Jesse's war record with a grain of salt. A man who would fib about railroad maps printed in black and white would as likely make up discharge papers from a guerrilla outfit the South never got around to recognizing as one of its own."

The barkeep looked sincerely puzzled as he asked what in thunder Jesse James might have to do with anyone this far west, insisting, "Last I read in the papers, the Younger brothers all seem to be dead or in jail, and nobody's seen hide nor hair of the James boys since that Northfield raid they messed up so bad. Some say one or both of 'em rode out of Northfield badly shot up. They haven't robbed nobody since. So who's to say they're not both dead, sort of sneaky?"

Longarm shrugged and said, "The Pinkertons, for one. They have more than one two-faced neighbor of Momma Zerelda on their own payroll. Rumor has it that while neither can go home to Momma right now, neither has moved that far from home. We've heard Frank James tried his hand at farming, which he should have stuck with to begin with, while Jesse's said to be posing as a horse trader. If we knew where or by what name we'd have him locked up with Cole Younger right now."

He sipped some suds and continued, "Other known business or drinking pards of the James and Younger gang have scattered wider. I nailed Cotton Younger, personal, in the Salt Lake City Federal Courthouse a spell back. I'm still working on any connection J. C. Ford of Denver might have had with the Ford boys suspected of riding with Frank and Jesse on occasion. He'd be too old to be another brother, today, even if the Denver Stranglers hadn't strung him up along with Black Hawk years ago. You said yourself that gold mines hold attractions for good old Southern boys, even when things might not be too hot for them in their old stamping grounds."

The barkeep nodded soberly and said, "Far be it from me to argue with the law if you say this Sweet William and Barbara Allan, related to the James boys, have been seen in these parts. But like I told you when you first came in, you're the first strange face I've served a beer to for a month of paydays, Deputy Long. For despite the way this camp might have got its name, it's been peaceable as all get out in these parts for many a year. All the fussing and fighting was back when there was still places to be sluiced or even panned from the headwaters of Clear Creek. Boys have a tougher time jumping one another's claims deep down in the blossom rock. You've seen our famous Glory Hole, haven't you?"

Longarm nodded and the local booster said, "There you go, then. The way the real professionals get rich is by working together, not murdering one another. The Glory Hole resulted when a half dozen separate mining outfits agreed to work together instead of against one another to get at the blossom rock under Quartz Hill. They packed all their mine shafts with dynamite, lit the fuses, and stood back, resulting in a swell hole a thousand feet across, and Lord knows how deep it'll be by the time they muck all the loose high grade and run it through the consolidated smelter built by good old Senator Nathaniel P. Hill. They make money up here in Gilpin County by thinking big, Deputy Long. What do you reckon a two-bit road agent like you're searching for in these parts would be doing in these parts to begin with?"

Longarm drained his schooner and put another nickel on the mahogany, saying, "Just one more and then I have to get it on down the road. If I knew what that petty but deadly young gunslick was planning in these parts I'd just stake it out instead of running about in circles like a big-ass bird. I haven't even figured what in thunder he thought he was doing up in Arnold Wells, where there's hardly anything at all worth stealing. He, or more likely that mystery woman he rides with, may have kin in Colorado. He may or may not be from Clay County, Missouri. We don't think she could be. Where would I go about buying me some henna rinse, in this town, if I wanted to color my hair red?"

The barkeep shot him a wary look, laughed like hell once he decided Longarm just couldn't be that sort of a gent, and replied, "Not here, for certain. You might try the druggist down by the gunsmith's."

Longarm brightened and decided, "I'll pay me a call on the gunsmith while I'm at it! For aside from her unusual hair fashions, one or more of 'em load up with mighty unusual ammunition as well!"

Suiting actions to his words he paid mere lip service to the full beer schooner he'd just paid for and left most of it on the bar as he stepped back outside, blinking in the sunlight now that said sun was staring down into the valley from a lot of mighty thin mountain air. He retraced his steps up the one main street, leading the barb by the reins until they came to an old cuss dozing in the doorway of a livery. Longarm bet him a dime that he didn't know how to rub down, water, and oat his pony, even if he unsaddled it himself. So the old-timer told him he'd lost, pocketed the drinking money, and Longarm was free to go on about his business in town afoot, even though he'd told Billy Vail time and time again that legwork was the most tedious part of this infernal underpaid job.

He was good at it, though, as Billy Vail had often told him. For part of the skills of a good tracker consisted of not running in one more circle than you had to. Seeing the way the gunsmith and drugstore were laid out, and seeing a fat and undecided-looking lady entering the drugstore, he crossed over to the gunsmith's instead.

The balding old gent who came out from the workshop in the back looked less annoyed at the disturbance after Longarm paid for two boxes of .44-40 rounds he could always use in any case. He hauled out his bitty brass derringer, unsnapped it from the end of his watch chain, and placed it on the glass between them to add, "This backup two-shooter could use new grips, or at least a new retaining screw, don't you agree, sir?"

The gunsmith picked up the little gun, got a bitty screwdriver out of the little leather tool kit in his own vest pocket, and fiddled with the derringer, saying, "You're right. You've stripped some threads here. Gun this size takes a hell of a beating firing man-sized rounds. You'd best let me drill these grips for a size larger screw. It'll cost you six bits."

Longarm agreed that sounded fair and asked if he could watch. The old man led him back to the cluttered workshop and removed the derringer grips entire as Longarm told him casually that he packed so much serious hardware because he packed a badge as well. The old-timer nodded curtly and didn't seem to care one way or the other as he said, "I had you figured for a shootist of serious intent on one side of the law or the other. In this business one can't afford to make moral judgments. Hardly any shoe clerks or Sunday-school teachers come to me with their problems, and I'm in this trade to make at least a modest living, you know."

As the older man inserted a grip in a wooden-jawed vise Longarm allowed he worked as hard as anyone might want to for his own pocket jingle, and went on in a more casual tone, "I'm up this way trying to cut the trail of a firearms enthusiast less inclined to honest toil than you or me, as a matter of fact."

The old gunsmith began to enlarge the screw hole with a hand-cranked tap as he replied, "Figured you had to be hunting somebody. Never took you for a gold prospector, and there's nothing much but color or crooks to hunt in these parts with all the timber cut and the game driven off by smelter stink. Doubt you'll find anyone to arrest here in Black Hawk, though. Company police have high-grading pretty much under control.

The ore's run right over to Central City for refining, and we don't even have our own bank yet."

Longarm said, "The young couple I'm hunting may be more interested in hiding out than drawing further attention to themselves. You'd know if you'd done any work on a Le Mat revolver or maybe sold some of that fancy French ammunition you need with one, wouldn't you?"

The old-timer grinned for the first time since Longarm had come in off the street and said, "Lord, I haven't seen a Le Mat for years. A mess of 'em were imported during the war by the Confederacy, the north having all them New England gun factories. J.E.B. Stuart was packing a Le Mat when the Yankees got him at Yellow Tavern. Some say Gray Ghost Mosby carried one as well. If so, he never bragged about it while he was organizing the Klan and trying to pass himself off as a military expert. I reckon a Le Mat was better than nothing. But nobody serious about his shooting would be packing one of them dumb French thumb-busters today."

Longarm held his own fire as the older man changed grips in the vise. Then he said, politely as possible, "You're wrong. William Allan, a suspected associate of Frank and Jesse James, packs at least two and maybe more Le Mats. His doxie, a lady known only as Barbara Allan, busted him out of jail in Arnold Wells with a brace of his or her own Le Mats. She killed two deputies in the process and each of 'em wound up seasoned with .40 caliber slugs and number-nine buck."

The old-timer nodded soberly and said, "That sounds like the sort of metal a Le Mat flings, true enough. Might have known someone as unusual as a homicidal female would be doing the flinging, though. The infernal hand cannon has awesomely poor balance, fires

80

slow as a cat shitting through a funnel, and to top it all off that freak French ammunition is hard as hell to come by. You see, it didn't matter so much in the cap-and-ball version, with each cased pistol coming with its own molds for casting your own shot and balls. But if we're talking postwar conversions, firing brass casing made to them odd French meter-measures—"

"Let's talk about that," Longarm cut in. "We've been sort of taking it for granted Allan and his doxie begged, borrowed or stole Le Mat conversions somewhere. Almost all the old Walker, Patterson, and New Haven hoglegs have been converted to brass instead of cap and ball by anyone still packing 'em."

The gunsmith nodded and said, "The conversion's cheap and simple, too. All you need is a new hammer and cylinder to fit into the same frame. Lots less dear than buying a new gun entire, even though I'd sure want double-action, myself, in this cruel modern world. This Allan rascal would still be better off if he sprung for a Colt Lighting, like they say Billy the Kid favors these days."

Longarm made a wry face and said, "There's another young asshole whose days are numbered, mark my word. But in fairness to The Kid, Sweet William Allan is less noted as a gunfighter than as a plain and simple killer who's done most if not all his killing with all the odds in his favor as well as a converted or old-fashioned Le Mat. Let's go over that one detail some more. It could be a heap of help to me if I knew for certain whether he has to get his ammo somewhere special, say a mail-order house."

The old-timer, having about finished his simple repair, began to put the derringer back together with a retaining screw one size up, saying, "I'd have to see one or more of the rascal's side arms to tell you anything for sure. But didn't you say he peppered them poor boys in Arnold Wells with .40 caliber slugs?"

As Longarm took his derringer back with a nod of thanks he said, "They no doubt find such weaponry tends to spook their victims. I recall a tale that might even be true about a lawman facing down a good-sized lynch mob with a brace of Le Mats. You can usually figure on plain old pistol rounds going about where they're aimed, but a shotgun barrel less'n a foot long has a mighty fickle-hearted look to it."

He snapped the sort of treacherous-looking derringer to his watch chain and tucked it back in his vest pocket as a sort of deadly fob as he added, "I still mean to ask along the way if anyone sells .40 caliber brass. Meanwhile, thanks to your tip, I'll be paying more attention to outlets where a conservative cuss may be able to pick up pillboxes of them loose-firing shotgun caps."

The gunsmith volunteered lots of general stores still stocked firing caps for the muzzle-loading bird guns lots of old boys still favored for really blasting ducks by the numbers. Longarm allowed he'd just said that, paid the old-timer for the merchandise, service, and advice, and let himself out.

It was going on high noon by now and even at this altitude the summer sun could beat down serious from a cloudless Colorado sky. So while he spied a couple of cow ponies tethered thoughtless down the street a piece, the plank walks and dusty ruts between were void of any other signs of life. He clunked on down to the drugstore, hoping that fat lady had cleared out by now. It appeared she had as he entered the cooler and darker shop to be greeted by no more than the tinkle of a bitty bell attached to the door above his dark Stetson. The tinkle brought a young gal wearing a white smock and auburn hair out from the back. As Longarm approached the fake marble counter from where she was regarding him, uncertainly, she licked her lips and warned him, "Dr. Sawyer just went home for his noon dinner, sir. But if there's anything you might need that is not of an, ah, delicate nature . . ."

He smiled and somehow managed not to say he never used 'em for the same reason he hated taking a bath with his socks on. So he got out his federal badge and I.D. to flash at her as he told her, "I could use some shaving soap, if you carry any that hasn't been stunk up with flowers. My true reason for pestering you, however, is that I'm on the trail of an outlaw traveling in the company of a fake redhead."

She laughed incredulously and assured him she was neither in the habit of associating with criminals nor inclined to have titian tresses, as she called 'em, by dishonest means.

He put his wallet away as he assured her he hadn't meant her, for land's sake, and explained more fully about the doleful events up at Arnold Wells. She said none of the young ladies she'd ever been allowed to associate with would do that, and then asked how Longarm knew they were talking about another gal who died her hair. When he blinked in surprise she explained, "We do sell henna powder, Deputy Long. It has other medicinal purposes and naturally we don't ask just what ladies who purchase it may wish to do with it. But I feel free to inform you that none of the, ah, unnatural redheads in Black Hawk could have been involved in that jailbreak up north or, come to think of it, out of town that long, doing anything."

Longarm said, "I knew I was grasping at straws when I came in here, ma'am. But I hope you can see why I'm pestering you like this. I can see from here your own hair springs from your pretty scalp as natural

83

as anything. But to keep her own hair so titian this other gal we're after must have to buy some of that henna stuff at least what, once a month?"

The lady druggist shook her red head to reply, "She'd want to use a rinse on it more often than that if she parts her hair in the middle like most of us. How often she'd have to buy henna powder would of course depend on how much she wanted to carry along with her. A year's supply wouldn't take up too much room in a carpet- or saddlebag." Then she asked, "Who said she used henna on her hair to begin with?"

Before Longarm could reply that bell behind him tinkled louder than anyone at all polite had any need to tinkle it, and so even before she gasped, "Oh, don't!" Longarm had rolled along the counter to wind up on one knee against a glass case with his six-gun out, and it was still close. For he and the son of a bitching backshooter in the doorway fired at the same time and the only edge Longarm had, or in this case needed, was a steadier aim under fire. The roughly dressed stranger in the doorway spanged two rounds into the place Longarm's spine had just occupied, while Longarm punched him just under the heart with a hot hunk of lead and deposited him faceup on the planking out front with his own smoking .45 and spurred boot heels on the jamb of the ajar door. As Longarm rose he heard hoofbeats out in the street. But by the time he got to the doorway all there was to be seen, at first, was a haze of settling dust in the middle distance. Those cow ponies he'd noticed earlier were no longer to be seen. Some two-legged curiosity seekers were, by this time. So he ducked back inside and began to reload as he called out, "Are you still with us, ma'am?"

He was more relieved than he let on when her now somewhat less neatly combed red hair appeared above the countertop, followed by a pair of green eyes wide enough to go with an owl, had owls hatched that pretty. She gasped, "Good heavens! What was that all about? What's happened to that man in our doorway?"

He reholstered his still-warm .44-40, saying, "About what he intended for me, albeit I'll thank you and everyone else to note he was hit from the front!"

She rolled gracefully over the counter, displaying just a flash of swirling petticoats and shapely ankles in high-buttoned shoes as she dashed past Longarm to hunker down by the silent form on the walk to feel for a pulse before she stared soberly back over one shoulder at Longarm to say, "I fear this poor mortal is dead, sir!"

He said, "Aw, my friends call me Custis, and I just told you I shot him because he was out to shoot me. Did you have wax in your delicate ears, just now, ma'am?"

Before she could answer Longarm, a skinny old goat with a steerhorn mustache that must have taken years to grow had joined them over the corpse with his Dragoon drawn and a tarnished badge pinned to the breast pocket of his soup-speckled black shirt. He whistled down at the dead man and asked Miss Mattie, as he called her, if she knew who'd done the dastardly deed.

Longarm was braced for a heap of confusion before he got things straight with the local law. But Mattie, bless her, just said, "I don't think I ever saw him around town before. I was serving this other lawman, here, when the loser simply popped into our shop and tried to shoot my customer in the back!"

The town law twirled one handle of his impossible mustache in a reflective manner as he mused aloud, "He didn't try half hard enough. You say you ride for the law, too, stranger?"

Longarm nodded, introduced himself, and got out his

I.D. to prove it, moving slow and sensible. When Sheriff Blake's deputy in Black Hawk made the connection he whistled again and opined, "We'll likely want to file this one as a suicide, you being the one and original Longarm and him striking me as no more than a saddle tramp with a mean disposition and no imagination!"

The girl didn't understand their drift as Longarm stared thoughtfully down at the shabby cadaver to reply, "I doubt he meant to stick up the drugstore. He and his sidekick had their ponies tethered just down the way. So they must have been watching the street from somewhere out of sight. If so, they saw a, ah, heavyset lady enter and leave here ahead of me. I wanted to give her time to leave as well, so I was in the gunsmith's up the way. That gave 'em at least a few minutes to rob Miss Mattie, here, with no witnesses worth mention. Yet they waited until I was inside with her, with my back to the street. Add it up."

The town law, whose name turned out to be Luke Farnsworth, still seemed reluctant to buy the squalid sudden shoot-out as a serious assassination attempt. He said, "Nobody's pegged a shot at me and I have to be better known to any crooks in these parts. So why would they want to gun a strange lawman from out of town?"

Longarm was too polite, and too smart, to point out the obvious motive. He meant to ask Sheriff Blake how come those shake-down Bummers were allowed to run so free in Central City, assuming he ever got back there alive. Deputy Farnsworth stepped back out into the sunlight to place two fingers somewhere under that monstrous mustache and sound a piercing whistle. As his own men moved in he turned back to Longarm to say, "It does sound open and shut. But you were planning on

86

sticking around 'til we could impanel a coroner's jury, right?"

Longarm said he would. He didn't want to. He knew he had to. The west sure had gotten formal about such matters since he'd first come out this way after the war.

Chapter 7

Longarm hated paperwork worse than digging post holes. But Billy Vail made him do so much of it that he knew he'd save a lot of time if he wrote up the depositions for Deputy Farnsworth, who seemed a mite confused about what happened next.

In filling out her version of the shoot-out, Mattie gave her full name as Matilda Joy Garner, age 24, single by reason of divorce, and that she worked part-time and dwelt just out of town, alone, in the cabin her mining man had bought for the two of them just before he'd run off with another woman.

None of this might have stuck in Longarm's head worth mention had Deputy Farnsworth and the local justice of the peace possessed the common sense of one piss-ant after they'd put their heads together. For the county seat was not only the logical place to hold a hearing on the demise of the mysterious gunslick, but a short lope away and possessed of handier food and shelter, Occidental or Oriental. Both would have been one hell of an improvement over the facilities of Black Hawk, where overnight transients seemed rare as hens' teeth, to hear them tell it when he asked about room and board for even one damned night.

But Farnsworth told Longarm it might be best if he hung around until they got official word from the county coroner, and Longarm felt less inclined to declare war over this after Miss Mattie allowed she could put him up for the night if he didn't mind a simple supper and muslin sheets on a tufted leather sofa.

He said he didn't. But it almost looked like she *meant* for him to spend the damned night on that damned sofa in her living room before they somehow wound up proving she was a redhead all over by the coal-oil light of her bedroom lamp.

She naturally felt obliged to carry on about it and ask how come he'd seduced her, once she'd had her wicked way with him, more than once. He'd long since learned that while female doctors, druggists, nurses and such who had both the know-how and whatevers to take care of themselves were almost as forward as menfolk, they still felt obligated to protest that no woman since Mother Eve had ever felt the simple urge to screw, and that all such indelicate behavior resulted from the lust of men, who were all alike.

He could have pointed out he'd just sort of drifted into bed with her with the current she'd set up by opening her damned door to him in the first place. But he knew that wasn't what she wanted to hear. So he held her naked body tighter against his and ran his free hand over her passion-flushed flesh to reassure her, as he might a spooked pony, while he told her it had no doubt been fated from the beginning of time, considering how

89

swell their private parts fit and how little effort either of them had made to wind up like this so early in the evening.

She snuggled closer and confided she felt it had to be fate, too, adding, "I swore I'd never forgive Elroy for running off on me like that with another woman. But somehow, right now, I don't have any hard feelings at all for him and that bitch."

But by the time he had a cheroot going for them to share in bed, she'd naturally gotten around to the hard feelings her missing husband had wanted to shove in that other woman, and she seemed to want Longarm to agree old Elroy had behaved mighty odd. So Longarm let her puff on the smoke as he assured her that any strange gal capable of screwing that much better than her sounded sort of frightening. He meant it. Old Mattie wasn't bad at all and anyone could see she was willing at mighty short notice. He didn't really want to think about how willing she'd been, how often, with any other horny cuss. So partly to change the subject and partly because he really cared, he took the cheroot out of her mouth to ask, "Could we talk some more about that outlaw gal I was asking you about when that rascal busted into our conversation so rude?"

She said, "I don't think Elroy ran off with any gal connected with that member of the James gang that you're hunting, darling. He vanished the winter before last, the brute, long before anyone ever held up that stagecoach with the help of a false-hearted woman."

Longarm took a drag on the cheroot, let it out his nostrils, and insisted, "Running off on even a wife as pretty as you don't amount to a federal crime, no offense. The lady known only as Barbara Allan has her own boyfriend, and we were talking about her hair coloring just before we both had to duck our heads a lot."

He let her have some smoke to study with as he added, "You were saying something about how much of that henna powder she could pack cross-country with her, remember?"

Mattie blew a whale spout of blue smoke at the rough-hewn rafters above them and replied, "I was about to ask you how you knew she did anything to her hair at all. As I was saying just before you somehow got a pillow under my poor little fanny, you brute, *my* hair is red all over with no help from any drugstore. Who told you this Barbara Allan gal uses artificial means in the first place?"

He snorted, "Hell, I got it from another gal who looked her over up close, and surely another gal would know, right?"

Then he wondered what he was snorting about as Mattie sniffed and told him, "Women with less interesting hair color are always prone to accuse us ladies of the titian persuasion of buying our beauty in a drugstore, whether they have any reason to suspect us or not."

He considered her words for two whole drags on his cheroot. For while the ash-blonde Regina Morpeth back in Arnold Wells had no sensible reason to be jealous of any other gal, as far as he could see, he was only a man and hence less likely to savvy the workings of female spite if he lived to be a hundred. He told the female he was with at the moment, "I confess I've yet to examine the hair of Barbara Allan, personal, at either end. But I do know natural red hair from the henna-rinsed kind, from across a saloon, whenever I spy it. So it seems to me that if a man can tell, at a distance, a woman standing closer—"

"Oh, don't be such a cowboy!" she cut in with an indulgent laugh. "Dance-hall girls *want* men to notice how artificial they look. It goes with the sale of artificial romance. You'd be surprised how many blondes and redheads there are, in polite society, who got their more natural beauty by way of chemistry."

He thought back, quickly decided old Regina had been a natural blonde, and said, "If I follow your drift, you're saying the mystery gal who busted Sweet William out of jail could be a whore of any color, so I could be wasting time pestering drugstores about her?"

She began to fondle him sort of sassy as well as friendly as she purred, "I'm glad you saw fit to pester me. You know how much I needed it. But when you're hunting other women try to remember how much easier it is for any of us to change our overall description, next to one of you poor dears."

He got rid of the cheroot, knowing she wanted him to, but still asked her to get to her point, if she was out to make one. So she told him, "That wicked gal you're asking about could be a natural redhead, a natural something else who just colored her hair long enough to bust her lover out of jail or, in sum, most any description of gal at all, right now. Wouldn't it make more sense for you to concentrate on finding someone who'd seen the *man* you're after, Custis?"

He said, "By Jimmies, you ought to come work for Billy Vail. For I could have been searching harder for the hole than I was the damned donut! William Allan don't describe half as interesting, but we do know a whole heap more about the background of the cuss. We've no reason at all to suspect the gal he threw in with after leaving Missouri of having any kith or kin back yonder. She could be anything from a run-off Kansas farmer's daughter to a Denver society wife with an unhealthy yen for adventure. I could be barking up dumb trees about Le Mat revolvers, too. Just before I met you, the gunsmith up the street told me my concerns for their ammunition supplies could be a mite overwrought. Where is it engraved in stone that either one of 'em just has to be packing such an unusual weapon, right now? After she got him out of the Arnold Wells jail they made considerable tracks, way down here to— Now that's sort of odd, too, once you study on it."

She had it half hard for him by now and seemed to be anxious to get it harder, judging from the way she was gripping it. But she still asked what was so odd and he told her, "Them coming back this way at all. They were less known up around Arnold Wells, since they'd never pulled anything there, yet Sweet William was still well known enough, *every* damned where, to get picked up by the law."

She sat up in bed to get a better grasp on the situation as she pointed out, not sounding really concerned, "She got him out of any trouble he was in up there, dear. So why are we worried about that bitty cow town?"

He replied, "We ain't. Don't jerk quite so hard unless you mean to discourage it. Some gents like painful loving. I don't."

She said he could hurt her, a little, if he wanted. So they forgot about Arnold Wells for a spell as he pounded her good and she allowed it didn't hurt at all. But later, after life's greatest but most fleeting pleasure had fled for at least another few minutes, she got him back on the subject of his other enthusiasms and he explained, "We're over a hundred miles, here, from Arnold Wells. If he was spotted by a small-town deputy there, where he'd never done anything, why in thunder would they want to run for Gilpin County, where they're downright famous! They got spotted smack in the railroad depot. Yet had they ridden a train that far in almost any other direction—"

"They have someone in these parts to hide out with," she cut in.

"That works better than some other things they might be planning. Sweet William's managed to get almost as much Wanted paper posted on him as Frank and Jesse together and so, like them, he's doubtless trying to drop out of the game for a cooling-down spell. Arnold Wells may have *sounded* like the sleepy surroundings a wanted man could settle down in with his sweet stuff for a spell, but it wasn't. A deputy called Dave Rice was too sharp eyed, or sharp eared. They say Sweet William was bragging in his cups just before his arrest."

She yawned and asked, "Why do you keep talking about that cow town they just ran off from, dear? Didn't you just chase them way down this way?"

He snuggled her closer and replied, "I'm trying to figure out why. Like I said, any other neck of the woods they could have gotten to by train in the same time makes more sense, unless, as you say, they have kith or kin in these parts. What would you say the population of this county might be, honey?"

She answered, "Good Lord, I can't even tell you who'd know! I suppose we could scare up a couple of hundred souls here in Black Hawk at a given time, but the faces would keep changing if you kept calling the roll. For few of the folk up here so high stay put from one year to the next. Mine managers, merchants, and of course the few farmers and stockmen tend to own their own property, library cards and such. Most of the miners and cowhands drift in and out with the other seasonal changes. Common-labor jobs in these mountains sound better to folk who've never spent a winter at this altitude."

He grimaced and said, "I've been snowed in a time or two." He didn't think she'd like to hear about the time

94

he'd been snowed in with no firewood, few blankets, and more than one woman, or how they'd all managed to keep warm enough to survive. So he said, "If Sweet William and his Barbara Allan mean to winter-over in these parts, it'll have to be with someone less fickle footed than summertimers. Unless they're spotted soon by someone else aside from my one old witness, I'll have to assume they've gone to ground in some infernal confederate's hidey-hole, say a cabin or abandoned try hole on private property."

She agreed there were a mess of both in them there hills and asked him to trim the lamp if he didn't feel like trying for another come. He figured there was sure to be another day before he got too old and feeble for a morning ride. So he yawned, then plunged her bedroom into darkness. But as he lay there trying to plunge on into the arms of Morpheus he couldn't help but notice she was crying fit to bust. She was trying to do so silently, but her attempts to stifle her damned sobs were shaking her whole damned bed. He sighed, reached out to her in the dark to haul her closer, and soothed, "Hell, I can get it up again if you want to that bad, honey."

She sniffed and confided, "I don't think I could take any more without some rest, Custis. For you're quite a man indeed, and nobody can say you don't know how to treat a lady. It's just that . . . no matter who else treats me right, and you know you weren't the first I'd hauled in here since it happened, I just can't get over the way *he* treated me, the sweet-talking son of a bitch!"

Longarm didn't ask who "he" might have been. He just lay still with one arm around her bare shoulders, letting her shake 'em all she needed to right now. He knew nothing he could say would really help because he figured he sort of knew how she felt, even though it had

95

never been a two-face *man* who'd left him feeling used, abused, and confused.

He fumbled for his shirt in the dark and got them another smoke going as she blubbered, half to herself, "I don't know why I can't just let go of the brute, Custis. I didn't hesitate to file the divorce papers after he'd been gone a full year. I swore then I'd never take him back if he came begging and I still say I wouldn't take him back if he came through yonder doorway this very minute. But how can I be sure I really mean it? He was the first man I ever gave myself to. Even after we were divorced I didn't really feel as if I'd ever belong to anyone but Elroy, and if he did come back, saying he was sorry, what would I ever do, darling?"

He tried not to laugh out loud as he told her, "I should hope the two of you would have the decency to wait until I could get dressed and out of the way. You did assure me you're not married up with any old boy who's apt to come busting in here, didn't you?"

She did laugh, albeit bitterly, and assured him, "Don't worry about Elroy coming back tonight or any other night, damn him. They say the harlot he'd been seeing on the side was no better than she should have been, but a real looker and, well, she must have been a better lay by far, right?"

He patted her bare shoulder, slid his hand a mite farther down her naked spine, and assured her, "Take the word of an older and wiser friend, Mattie. There just ain't that much difference in human anatomy or the way one uses the same. Nine out of ten folk are worth going to bed with and the tenth is worth it for the novelty. If you've been fishing to be told you're a great lay, consider yourself told."

"Then why did Elroy run off with that whore?" she demanded. "He could have had her, all three ways for

96

two dollars, according to the stories the other men in town told about her."

Longarm yawned and started to say something banal about grits sounding tempting after a gent had been stuck with steak and spuds night after night. But he found himself interested despite himself. He frowned thoughtfully and decided aloud, "Men seldom run off with a downright professional woman unless she's got something to offer they just can't get anywhere else. You say this other gal could pleasure a man sort of perverse if he made it worth her while?"

She replied indignantly, "I don't see how she could have gotten much pleasure out of it, herself. But I've always been a good sport about such matters, and as I'd told Elroy more than once, it didn't bother me, once he'd gotten it in, back there. Would you like me to show you how down and dirty I can get with a man, darling?"

He laughed and said, "You may be sorry you made that offer before you're rid of me in the cold gray dawn, little darling. But now you really have my hunting instincts up. For I feel from sweet personal experience that your man had no sensible reason to run off like that and leave his property as well as you behind. Tell me more about this shady lady who tempted him down such a dumb as well as primrose path."

She sighed and said, "I've told you all I know. I never met the low-life siren. She worked at a dive over in Central City and I didn't even know Elroy had been buying drinks for her until later, after he'd run off with her. He told *me* those trips over to the county seat had something to do with the mining business. How was I to know it was monkey business? What do you suppose she *did* for him, Custis? Would you like me to show you how deep I can swallow it, hard, without gagging?"

He started to say no. Then he wondered why he'd

want to say a dumb thing like that. For life was short, his tool was sort of long, and most gals did tend to gag if you really let yourself go with 'em that way. So as long as she wanted to show off how free and easy she could get with a man, he graciously allowed her to treat him to a French lesson in depth and then, since she still wanted to show off, he indulged her in some so-called Greek loving, so called because more than one gal had assured him nobody went in for it like high-toned gents who'd been sent off to fancy boarding schools, albeit most state prisons afforded the same social advantages.

Longarm had been raised natural enough to enjoy anything that didn't hurt. So having proven that she could take it any way any infernal gold-camp whore could, they finished right and he told her sincerely, "Your man never ran off in search of a prettier face or a hotter body, honey. You say he was a mining man, here in Black Hawk, yet he had lots of business over in the next camp?"

She insisted, "Monkey business. Elroy worked as a drill foreman for the Black Hawk Mining Company. He had to know something about geology to follow the blossom rock as it twisted and turned through the dumb granite down below. But he wasn't following his own vein, and unless he was high-grading on the sly he had no call to do business with anyone over to the county seat, right?"

Longarm said, "I can't rightly say, just guessing. Remind me to put his name and the name of that fancy gal and so on in my notebook, come morning. As long as I have to wander all over the county asking other dumb questions, I may as well see if I can find out what made your man act so odd."

She rolled atop him to rub all over him in a surprisingly sisterly way as she sort of sobbed, "Oh, would you, Custis? Could you, Custis? It's not that I ever want to see the brute again, it's just that . . . Oh, shit, you know I want him back so bad I can taste it, don't you?"

He sighed and said, "Yeah. I've been there, kid. More than once, so I can tell you time and time alone is the only salve that'll heal such hurts. One time I found a gal I was mighty fond of dead and mutilated Indian style on the North Plains. I lost track of how much Maryland rye I drank, or how many sweet young things I tried to try to forget old Roping Sally. In the end the hurt just faded away to a burnt spot on my heart I only notice now and again, like right now. You'll meet other men, more important to you than I was tonight, and you'll likely suffer other hurts and then, in time, you'll be able to forget your first love for, oh, days at a time."

She sighed and said, "I hope you're right. I think it's the not knowing that gets my teeth to really grinding, Custis. I think if I knew how on earth she got my man away from me I might be able to live with it and even wish 'em luck. For I just can't think of anything she could have done with Elroy that I'd want to do with him or any man!"

He laughed, patted her some more, but didn't answer and, as he'd hoped, the lack of conversation after all that unexpected exercise had her sound asleep in no time.

As he lay there in the dark, in a strange bed, listening to a pretty stranger softly snoring, he knew he wasn't going to drop off for quite a spell, damn his own curious mind.

It wasn't the strangeness of his surroundings. He'd gotten to where he sort of enjoyed a change of scene as well as females to share it with. He was keyed up because he had just too many damned balls in the air at once.

99

Billy Vail had sent him to bring in Sweet William and, all right, Barbara Allan as well, since the two of them seemed to be a set the Justice Department wanted wrapped up together. So why in thunder was he concerned about local thugs shaking down his Chinese friends and why, for God's sake, had he just offered to locate a wayward husband with at least a two-year lead on him?

Knowing just what Billy Vail would say about him wasting even that much thought on affairs the federal government had no interest at all in, Longarm muttered, "Well, what if Sweet William and his doxie are hiding out with local crooks, and what if my stirring up local crooks leads to something I *should* be interested in?"

So now he could even hear that fool Henry laughing at him and sneering, "Nice try, Romeo. Only when are you fixing to start thinking with your brains instead of your cock and balls?"

Chapter 8

As Longarm could have told them in Black Hawk, but felt just as glad he hadn't, the county coroner had sent back word by morning that all they needed was the deposition of a federal officer, for God's sake, and the I.D. of the dead suspect, if available. The death of total strangers with no kith or kin who voted in or about Gilpin County was hardly worth the expense to the honest taxpayers of a full and formal hearing. A copy of a properly made out death certificate, along with Longarm's word and the backup deposition of Matilda Garner, a resident of the county wanted for neither lying nor stealing in the past, was good enough for now.

So Longarm was on his way back to Central City before noon, feeling even gladder after Mattie had seen him off with French toast for breakfast and old-fashioned loving on the kitchen table afterwards.

The two mining camps were so close together it was

safe to assume that in times to come they'd sort of wind up being one bigger and even more sloppy township, albeit it was tough to see how the country between 'em right now could get much more torn up. Any vegetation worth using as a mine prop, stuffing in a stove or feeding a damned goat had long since vanished, leaving the rusty railway and rutted dirt road to wind through slopes the same shade of soot and fly-ash-dusted mud. The black crud that settled blew down the slopes from the smelters great and small of Central City.

Here and there rose the soot-stained stone foundation or even the chimney of an abandoned dwelling, steam hoist, or whatever. It was hard to tell because the lumber of any abandoned structure was cannibalized almost at once to build something else, somewhere else, in the mighty shifty scenery of gut-and-git mining country. Big piles of lighter mine tailings staining the darker dead soil all around told of crushed dreams as well as crushed granite. For gold was where one found it, and even here in perhaps the richest few square miles of the west the fickle veins could swell to trainloads of soft blossom rock for the scooping with a spoon or pinch out to nothing in the harder granite within yards or, hell, inches. Ninety-nine out of a hundred so-called abandoned mines in mining country were actually "try holes," or exploratory shafts yielding little more than blood, sweat, and tears. Blood flowed easily and often senselessly wherever Mother Earth bled precious metal. Men sweated to get at it whether it was there or not. The tears came for both obvious and not so obvious reasons. Many a man had died broke after a lifetime thrown away on the search for color, whether color had been found or not. Old Sutter had been ruined by the discovery of gold in the mill race he was really asking them to dig for him, and he hadn't been the first to learn that a man's troubles could just be starting with such sudden surprises. Longarm was glad he'd never really come down with gold fever. He'd arrested too many men who had before even trying to pan any, just for the hell of it, himself. Like the lawyers who got richer at the study of mining law, a lawman had to know more than many prospectors about the profit and loss figures that went into the game. Most folk figured all you had to do was strike gold in your back yard and all your troubles were over. Longarm had seen too many men die at the hands of claim jumpers or the law to buy that simple notion. Mattie had said her man had only been a mine worker, not an owner. Her remark about him being a possible high-grader was no doubt inspired by the way he'd betrayed her own trust in him. It hardly seemed likely he'd been eliminated by the company police as a high-grader. They tended to make sure everyone heard about it when and if they caught a high-grader. For it wasn't often they did, and the temptation around ore as easy to high-grade as blossom rock was said to tempt saints.

Longarm heeled his borrowed mount into a trot to get it past some runoff water puddled in the road. There was arsenic as well as gold in them there hills, and livestock only knew the damned stuff made water taste sweet.

As he left the danger behind he reflected that the try hole it had run down from had likely held at least some color. Nobody dug all that deep without any encouragements at all. The trouble was that the very thing that made blossom rock so easy to high-grade made it easy to waste one hell of a heap of sweat on.

Most gold ore, in other parts of the west, looked just like the damned old rock you used for railroad ballast. It was hard as granite, and the color in it was seldom visible to the naked eye. You found it with a streak test if you'd found gold indeed, or more fancy chemical tests if it was there but not as anxious to come out. Once you knew you had rock worth mucking you crushed it fine as a lady's face powder and the chemistry just got started. But blossom rock was the stuff prospectors' dreams were made of.

It was the source of most placer gold, washed out of it by frost and rain to settle farther down the slopes in streambeds, and in essence consisted of gold-bearing quartz that had been rotted soft as brick by ground-water chemistry Longarm saw no need to worry about. The point was that nothing rotted gold. So any gold in the blossom rock, from dust to nuggets too heavy for one man to lift, were just there, to be dug out of the soft crud. Most of it, of course, was almost too fine to see. So even though the refining of blossom rock was duck-soup simple, next to, say, telluride, most of the gold was extracted that way. Bigger nuggets were supposed to be turned over to the company, as well, and the company police tended to pat men down for raw gold or "high grade" as they came off shift. But there were ways. If all else failed a high-grader could simply swallow a few hundred dollars' worth. Gold wasn't poisonous, came out sooner or later, and could be sold to any crooked pawnbroker for the going rate of ten dollars an ounce out the asshole, or twenty an ounce at the Denver Mint with the proper papers.

As he already spied occupied cabins on the outskirts of Central City, ahead, Longarm told himself to set aside the notion of high-grading husbands for now. The odds were as good that he'd really run off with that other gal. As a lawman he'd learned better than to even wonder why some men seemed willing to turn themselves inside out for a gal who looked downright plain to others. He had the handle of the trashy dance-hall gal in his notebook. If it didn't lead him too far from the line of duty, he meant to see if he could match up the time she left town for parts unknown with the time old Elroy vanished. Mattie had said herself that folk came and went a heap in these parts, and she was likely to feel she'd been mighty uncharitable if the drab showed up just as drab in some other mining camp, performing the same services old Elroy could have had without eloping with her.

He told himself not to think about Bummers shaking Chinese folk down for protection money, either, albeit it got harder not to think about the swell screwing he'd been served after that otherwise bland Chinese dessert. As he caught himself comparing Oriental and Occidental anatomy, noting with a grin that it wasn't really true what they said about Chinese girls, he told himself to damn it cut that out and gave his barb a good hard kick to lope it the rest of the way into town.

The spunky short-spined Spanish pony threw itself forward with a will, and so it would be up for grabs, later, as to whether Longarm or his frisky mount had saved the day. For, either way, the unexpected movement ruined the aim of the bushwhacker up the slope, and by the time he or she could get off a second shot Longarm and his Winchester had rolled off the far side and kept rolling while the spooked pony lit out for town and the comforting corral it had come from to begin with.

Longarm was glad it hadn't rained recent as he crabbed sideways on his tweed-covered knees and elbows with the carbine cradled in his arms on the safer side of the railroad bank. The narrow-gauge line hadn't been ballasted more than a yard or so higher than the service road Longarm had just been riding, so there was no way to run upright behind it. He could only crawl well clear of the place he'd first rolled over before he removed his hat and raised his head for a look-see.

He flattened his cheek to the dusty ballast as a big rifle ball spanged off a cross-tie and howled its anguish to the empty air behind him. Longarm grinned wolfishly as the reason for the slow rate of fire sank in. A .50 caliber ball from a buffalo rifle, likely a Sharps, was dreadful to get hit with, but had its own distinctive ricochet. Longarm had spotted the cotton puff of black powder smoke way up the slope, or he might not have ducked in time. He moved back the way he'd just come from and risked the crown of his hat, this time. Again the distant rifle roared and this time Longarm didn't duck. He was on his feet and charging across the tracks, firing his repeating Winchester from the hip, and then he'd made it to a rainwater gully cut deep into the clay soil on the uphill side of the road before the sniper could reload his long-range, high-powered, but *single-shot* rifle.

As Longarm shucked his frock coat to worm up the deep but skinny gully, another big buffalo round shot a shovelful of grit and dust skyward, up the slope a good dozen yards, or about where Longarm would have been by now if he hadn't paused to get rid of his coat. The unknown bushwhacker had likely done this sort of thing before. It was sort of sobering to consider he was still alive, meaning he'd not only done it before but won.

Longarm stayed put by his bunched-up coat and, sure enough, more dust rose even farther up the gully. The rifleman had to know he couldn't nail anyone who stayed down in the slot. The idea was to make sure nobody popped up out of it. There could only be one purpose. Longarm had played this same deadly game in the past and he was still alive as well. So he waited 'til yet another shot rang out. Then he rose to his own feet

106

and fired as, sure enough, a raggedy figure was running from one old dugout to the spoil pile of another, higher up.

Longarm knew from the way his target's hat flew up and backwards that he'd scored a spine shot. But as he charged on up the gritty slope he pumped another round into the son of a bitch he'd dropped, just for old time's sake. So as he kicked the limp body over on its back and hunkered down for both cover and a look-see, he could see at once the rascal was dead. It only took a second longer to decide he was sure about that dirty unshaven face. It was the same unwashed lout he'd hauled off the fair body of the Widow Lee!

As he patted the body down for I.D. Longarm muttered, "I've heard of sore losers, but you really won yourself the booby prize, didn't you?"

He found a surprisingly neat and expensive leather billfold in the dead man's hip pocket. He muttered, "Dumb place to carry your wallet, too." Then he opened it, blinked at the little gilt badge and I.D., then whistled and added, "Your agency sure doesn't train its help as good as Pinkerton does. One of the first rules is never mess with a real lawman, and the second is never mess with any man who's already shown you he's tougher than you are, or were, you poor simp!"

He caught movement out the corner of one eye and rose to get back down to his coat before someone could steal it. The sounds of gunplay had inspired quite a crowd to come out across the clay slopes from the outlying shanties of Central City. Most of them seemed to be mean little kids and even meaner looking dogs. But as he beat them all to his coat in the gully and bent down to pick it up, a full-grown gent with a county badge visible on his faded old army shirt tried not to look as worried about Longarm's Winchester as he must have been, demanding, "What's going on here? Do you know who's been doing all that shooting, and why?"

To which Longarm replied with a thin smile, "The shooting's over. I'm still working on the why."

Filling some pages of his notebook with barefaced facts of public record caused Longarm to eat his noon dinner a mite late that day. But thanks to Sheriff Blake asking the file clerks in the county courthouse not to fuck with their federal guest, Longarm got his chili con carne and apple pie before one P.M.

He'd picked up the pony and his more important personal saddle and possibles right after he'd ridden into town with the body on a buckboard. But he didn't go back to Hong Lee Mao's for another swell meal. Whether he meant to have supper there or not had a lot to do with how his next social call might or might not go.

The Peerless Saloon stood catty-corner at an awkward angle from the otherwise innocent chili parlor. So leaving his barb tethered on the shady side of the same he legged it on over, Winchester and all. But as he parted the batwings with his reloaded carbine's muzzle, he saw that nobody much seemed to be laying for him inside. The cool, dimly lit interior revealed a quartet of gents playing poker at a corner table, a painted but ugly gal at the bar in a red and black outfit with its skirts cut rainy-susan, and of course the one-eyed barkeep regarding him with displeasure as he bellied up to the bar a safe distance from the whore, placed his Winchester on the mahogany in front of him, and said, "I don't want a drink. I want a word with the owner, and before you tell me he ain't here I'd best advise you I'm the law, federal, and that they just told me over at the courthouse that he lives on the premises, just upstairs."

The barkeep shrugged and said, "You don't know everything. We got our own friends in high places. So we knew you were coming, Longarm." Then he told the whore to take Longarm upstairs to Squire Tierney. So he had to follow her, resisting the impulse to tell her he just wasn't that sort of boy. She didn't look as awful from the rear. But she didn't look all that great, either, no matter how she tried to swing that skinny behind on the way up the stairs.

Squire Tierney, as he wanted folk to call him, turned out to be a friendlier looking cuss than Longarm had expected, once the dismal-looking gal had left them alone in a sort of combination office and front parlor, overlooking the street. Tierney was somewhere in his late forties or early fifties, still husky but commencing to go just a mite to pot in his conservative snuff-colored suit and flashy silk vest of emerald green with Celtic crosses embroidered all over it in gold. He sat Longarm down in a comfortable chair by the lace-curtained window and poured them both what he described as "A taste of the real creature," before sitting down across from Longarm with the bottle on the windowsill between them. Longarm sipped cautiously with his Winchester across his knees and a casual eye on the one door in or out. The gracious crime lord of Central City didn't seem to have any gun more serious than a derringer on him. But he was said to possess a vile as well as uncertain temper under that bland exterior. As if to prove it, the burly Irishman smiled wolfishly across at Longarm to purr in a queer mixture of blarney and bare-fanged menace, "You can see Pablo's chili parlor indeed from me front windows, and some of the boyos are quite cross with you about the way you dealt with two of our dear friends, Longarm. But it's an easygoing gent I've ever been, and I told them we'd best be hearing your side of it before we took further steps in the matter."

Longarm set his Waterford glass on the sill by the bottle, having taken enough of a sip to avoid deliberate challenge, and said, "I'm not about to waste good wind trying to justify the killings of those two killers. Whether I have to kill you or not depends a lot on how good a listener you are, you larcenous but so-far-not-federal asshole."

Tierney put his own drink aside as he quietly observed he didn't like to be called an asshole. So Longarm replied, "Quit acting like one, then. The state of Colorado takes high-grading serious as hell, and the Mine Owners' Association can get downright murderous on the subject. But you and your boys should have known right off that the U.S. Justice Department's never been invited to police private property up here in Gilpin County."

Tierney looked more sick to his stomach than angry as he quietly asked who might have accused anyone hereabouts of high-grading. To which Longarm replied as quietly, "Nobody had to tell me. I just said I was up here on a federal case, but give me credit for working some things out when they're shoved in my face like dirty socks. A spell back I did get to track down some high-graders out California way because the mine they were robbing had a contract with the U.S. Mint. But I only work serious on serious cases, and if I tried to clean up all the high-grading in this land of opportunity I'd never get anything else done. High-grading goes with mining the same as whores, gamblers and strikes. In blossom rock lodes like they're mining around here it gets even worse. But what the hell, I might be tempted, my ownself, if I was drawing the going rates for hard-rock mucking and I suddenly saw a month's pay in raw gold sticking out of the rock at me while I was alone in the tunnel."

"Do I look like a hard-rock, or hell, a soft-rock miner?" grumbled Tierney.

"Nope. You're one of the receivers of stolen goods the boys unload their purloined nuggets and wire-gold on. Before you cloud up and rain all over me, I repeat it's none of my federal business and, as a matter of fact, I suspect some of my best friends in Central City buy stray gold at ten and sell down Denver way for twenty. You ought to learn to live and let live, Irish. Sending that animal, Grady, to demand a cut from the Widow Lee was dumb enough. Letting him start a war with me just for making him stop was even dumber."

Tierney stared out the window as if he expected the mighty dull scenery out yonder to move as he asked, innocently, who on earth Longarm could be talking about.

Longarm snorted in disgust and said, "Joseph O'Bannion Grady is reposing at the moment in the Central City Morgue, along with one Kevin Cassidy who tried to back-shoot me yesterday in Black Hawk. I don't blame you for wanting to avoid the funeral costs. But I just came from the county clerk's, and while Cassidy was too old a pro to pack real I.D., the two of them had both applied for company police licenses, and gotten them."

He reached under his coat for a cheroot as he continued, smiling softly, "I wonder how the M.O.A. would take it if they heard a couple of gun hands they'd hired to control high-grading were in fact in cahoots with you and shaking down others in the trade. They do have some really high-paid gun hands on tap for *serious* work, I hear."

Tierney didn't sound as scared as his complexion

111

gave away as he blustered, "I don't have anything to hide. If Joe Grady was pestering some fool Chinese about anything it was on his own. I hadn't heard about him having trouble with a U.S. deputy, and if I had I surely never would have told him to go after such dangerous quarry with no more than poor old Kevin backing his play!"

Longarm lit his smoke before he nodded pleasantly and said, "I'm choosing to believe that, because it works out best for both of us if you'd rather act like a public-spirited citizen. Like I said, trading in high grade is no more a federal crime than selling wine, women, and song at outrageous prices. I can be as live-and-let-live as any county sheriff as long as nobody tries to kill me or fuck up a case I'm really out to crack. How do you like it so far?"

Tierney smiled cautiously and replied, "Name it. Is it wine, women, or song you'd enjoy, on the house?"

Longarm smiled back and said, "Just some singing. Is it true you served in the war with the New York Sixty-ninth?"

The burly Irishman scowled and said, "I did, and it's nothing to be ashamed of, for it was a grand fight we put up at Gettysburg for lads just off the boat, and what's it to you?"

Longarm said, "The road agent I'm hunting may have kin in these parts who got here earlier and fought on the other side. His name is William Allan and I'm pretty sure that's an English name, by the way."

Tierney grimaced and said, "I heard about that stage robbery more than a year ago. I heard the road agent and his Barbara Allan may be back in town, as well. After that your guess is as good as mine. I've yet to set eyes on the rebel of Saxon blood who gunned a shotgun messenger named Nolan and all and all."

Longarm flicked some ash out the window as he pondered a mite before deciding, "Neither Grady nor Cassidy had any Confederate connections, and I said I was willing to buy your story for now. But just between you, me, and yonder lamppost there can't be much skulduggery going on in these parts that you're not party to. So I want you to put out the word that we *want* that murderous pair, wherever they may be holed up around here, and that when we catch 'em, and we always do, it'll go hard on anyone we find aiding and abetting 'em, long-lost kin or not."

Tierney nodded soberly and said, "Consider it done. For while I'm as live-and-let-live, it's true I have ways of finding things out, if I set me mind to it and all and all."

Longarm said, "Bueno. I'll check back with you from time to time as I do some more questioning on my own."

He hesitated, knowing Billy Vail would hardly approve, then he shrugged and said, "As long as we're jawing about this and that so freely, Irish, they tell me you used to have a wild and wicked beauty working here who answered to the handle of Kerry Rose. True?"

Tierney smiled fondly and didn't seem evasive as he replied, "I did, and while I usually don't mix business with pleasure, the dear girl was too grand a temptation to pass up. I'd have been willing to set her up as me own private stock, to tell the truth. But Kerry Rose was one of them rare ones who enjoyed her work. Fifteen men she was after taking on atop the bar downstairs in a row, one night, and every one of 'em in love with her in the end. You see, she had this innocent way of smiling all the while, as if it was just good clean fun and . . . aragh, what about her, then? Last I heard she was running her own place over in Steamboat Springs, and doing a land-office business as well, to nobody's great surprise."

Longarm frowned and said, "Now that's real odd, assuming someone ain't fibbing like hell. For I had it on good authority that a mining man named Elroy Garner ran off on his wife and property with the one and only Kerry Rose. Having met the wife I feel safe to assume Kerry Rose was as tempting as everyone says."

The vice lord laughed incredulously and insisted, "It's a madam she is in Steamboat Springs, I tell you. Why would I lie, and for that matter why would Kerry Rose be giving it all to one mere man when it's a dozen a night at least she needs to satisfy her great passion?"

Longarm grimaced at the picture and decided, "Someone has that vanishing act of Elroy Garner wrong as hell, then. I wish I had time to go into it more. But you can only eat the apple a bite at a time and . . . Could you put out some feelers on that for me as well, old pard?"

Tierney laughed dryly and said, "Let's not be overdoing it. I never heard of the love sick fool, if he was an admirer of Kerry Rose. But then, who was after counting? Some of the boyos may know who it is you're asking about. But I take it Sweet William and Barbara Allan are the ones you're really anxious about?"

Longarm said that was about the size of it and added he'd be back at the Blossom Rock Hotel as they shook on it friendly, he hoped.

Longarm spent the greater part of that afternoon back at the courthouse, getting really dusty mouthed pawing through dry papers without as much luck as he'd had that morning.

As he'd already known, tempers had flared some in the Colorado mining country during the war, less than a generation back, and the Colorado Militia had been almost as rough on "copperheads," as those siding with the south had been called, as they'd been on the South Cheyenne. It was naturally safe to say as many old grudges were still being nursed in Gilpin County, Colorado, as Clay County, Missouri, albeit in reverse. So what in thunder could have drawn Sweet William back here?

It had to be something more attractive to a wanted killer than just a place to hole up. The very factors that made it so easy for the James and Younger clan to fade into the wooded hills of Missouri worked directly against even a fringe member of the clan out here in unreconstructed Yankee range. He pawed through the records in vain for evidence of anyone from Missouri or, hell, anywhere the Stars and Bars had ever flown, filing any claim for anything in Gilpin County. If that murderous young couple were holed up with kith or kin within a day's ride, they'd shown up after the war under false colors. But, of course, there was a lot of that going around in a land where one just never knew which side a bitter-faced gent at the bar might have ridden for.

Yet even assuming one or more property owners in the neighborhood were secret southerners, it was still the wrong kind of neighborhood for any kith or kin of the James boys to hole up in. Billy Vail had often said, and Longarm tended to agree, that if even one of the country folk in and about Clay County got seriously sore at Frank or Jesse they'd be killed or captured in no time. To have lasted as long as they had, the Missouri owlhoots had to have enjoyed the good will of every neighbor for miles around. It hardly seemed possible the mostly Yankee country folk of Colorado could be counted on to present a solid front against the law for

115

anyone even possibly related to anyone who'd ridden with Quantrill!

Looking for other names entire Longarm came across that of old Elroy Garner more than once, cuss his uncertain fate. Longarm saw Mattie had told him true about the dates of their marriage and divorce on grounds of cruel desertion. He hadn't thought she was lying about her man, whether others had lied to her about Elroy and Kerry Rose or not. He found out what Elroy *might* have been up to riding over here to the county seat so often when he finally got around to a drawer's worth of mineral claims, having exhausted county cattle brands in search of southern sympathies. Nobody named Allan, James, or Younger seemed to own a mine or even a try hole within miles. But there was old Elroy Garner's claim to the usual plot of hillside fifty-by-one-hundred-feet wide. Interested despite what Billy Vail might have to say about it, Longarm carried the loose sheet out front to where a plump but sort of pretty file clerk sat filing her nails to ask if there was any way to locate this mysterious gold strike on a map, explaining, "The missing man who filed it was working at the time for the Black Hawk Mining Company, so what business might he have had filing on his very own mine?"

The fat girl must have thought he was sort of pretty, too. For she jumped right up and led him into yet another storeroom where they kept maps and mine layouts neither rolled nor folded, in big flat drawers. She read off the plat number Garner had put down as his own and bent over, sort of tempting, to slide out a big county survey map she said that number went with. As they stood side-by-side to examine her find atop the cabinet, it was she who found it first, of course. But naturally she had no notion why Longarm gasped, "Thunderation!" until he explained to her, "If this is one corner of

116

Black Hawk, in this corner, Elroy Garner wanted permit to dig for color right *here*, just upslope and over one modest ridge from the cabin he shared with his red-headed woman, down *this* way, see?"

The fat girl nodded and said, "What of it? Lots of mining men prospect during their time off. I don't mind telling you it makes some of 'em dull boyfriends indeed. I once packed a picnic basket for a swain who left me half the durned afternoon on a hilltop while he poked about in old try holes, can you imagine?"

He didn't know her well enough to ask which hole she might have wanted the poor sap to try. He just said, "You're no doubt as well off without such a stupid swain, ma'am. I can see how finding one's own gold mine has to have working in one beat by miles, but it seems to me a try hole would be about as dumb a place to look as any I can come up with. If anyone had found color there they'd have never just walked away from their hole in the hill, right?"

She sighed and said, "Not always. My daddy is a mining man, albeit not nearly so rude, so I do know a little about seeking color and, you see, they hardly ever dug at all without at least suspecting there was something worth digging out."

He nodded and insisted, "That's about what I just said, ain't it? Somebody sunk a shaft where the rock looked promising and then gave up when they failed to find anything. According to this map, most of the slopes above Black Hawk are already riddled with abandoned claims from the earlier prospecting. So it's small wonder old Elroy vanished shortly after filing this fool claim. He must have felt too foolish to go home, once he sobered up."

She shifted her weight from one foot to the other, as if she had to pee, wanted a chance to speak up, or both. So he let her have her say and she said, "It's true the hills all around are honeycombed with abandoned try holes. Kids are always falling down them and they say bears den up in them as well. But most of 'em were sunk back in the fifties and sixties, right after old Johnny Gregory panned close to a thousand dollars' worth of Clear Creek placer in less'n four full days. It wasn't many days after that they found out where all that placer was coming from, and blossom rock veins are easy to dig as well as easy to spot."

He nodded and said, "I know a little about prospecting. Whether you find gold in rotten quartz or not depends on whether there was gold or no gold in it while it was still molten quartz. If there had been where old Elroy Garner sought it just up the mountain from his cabin, any one of these earlier try holes polka-dotting this here map would have struck smack into it long ago. You'd think a drilling foreman like Garner would have known that, for Pete's sake."

She said, "I'm sure he did, now that you've told me he knew more than most about mining. The earlier prospectors who combed these hills for cream to skim didn't know as much about color as *I* do, and even I know that for every ton of blossom rock in these hills there has to be a hundred tons of *telluride*!"

Longarm whistled as that sank in. He said, "I hope you're wrong. I just don't have the time to reopen a missing-person case that could turn out to be murder for— Hold on, wouldn't there be some other claim made out to the same fifty by one hundred infernal feet if old Elroy had had this one bought, won, or stolen off him?"

She said there might be something like that in the files. So the two of them went back to that smaller darker room and got all sweaty searching side-by-side for evidence of foul play before he was forced to agree

118

nobody had wound up with Elroy Garner's gold, if he'd ever found any, and that her suggestion about a shower bath sounded downright heavenly. But whether she'd meant together or separate he had to tell her, "I've just got time, if I start right now. For I have to get out to that missing man's claim before sundown lest me and my whole horse wind up missing as well."

She pouted out her lower lip, said she'd no doubt be off for the day before he could get anywhere near that dumb old try hole, and added it seemed just her luck that every nice-looking man she met in these damned mountains seemed to want to probe old holes full of mud and spiders instead of . . . never mind.

So he kissed her smack on the lips and told her, "I ought to get back before midnight, if you'd like to come up to my hotel room with me, honey."

He wasn't surprised when she gasped, turned beet red, and demanded to know what had given him the notion she was that kind of girl. So he said he was sorry, but tried to kiss her again, and grinned sort of crafty when she slapped his face, not too hard, and ran out of there blushing and giggling, pleased as punch. For he owed the poor critter for the real help she'd given him and, what the hell, it took so little to please some gals, if a man was only willing to be a good sport.

Chapter 9

It was as short a ride as ever, but Longarm still reined in
way downslope and tied up to a telegraph post by the
railroad line. It hadn't gotten all that dark when the afternoon sun had sank behind a purple ridge to the west,
but it *could* be getting dark by the time he was ready to
ride back down, and a man had to think ahead in try-
hole country. It wasn't the holes you could see right off
that did you in, he knew. Some sons of bitches had left
their entrances half screened by mud-coated planks and
fireweed. He made good time trudging up toward old
Elroy's mysterious claim with an improvised map in one
hand and his Winchester in the other. A couple of times
he stopped abruptly and spun around. But each time he
did all he saw was his ever-shrinking pony way down
the bare open slope he'd negotiated so far. He had no
idea why the hairs on the nape of his neck were tingling
like that. He had no reason to suspect he'd been fol-

lowed from Central City, and he hadn't wired anyone in Black Hawk, even Mattie, that he was coming. Yet he still felt spooked about something, and he'd learned as a teenager at a place called Shiloh that Mother Nature had put those tingle-hairs there for a damned good reason. They generally meant it was time to duck. He lit a smoke and moved on, muttering, "I *would* duck, damn it, if there was any cover to duck behind or if there was anything bigger than a horny toad within rifle range, you fool hairs!"

He went over the ridge he'd already noticed on the survey map. The hillsides this far up had commenced to heal a mite since the last time they'd been combed for pit props and firewood. Bunchgrass grew ungrazed amid fair-sized aspen sprouts all around. For nobody with a lick of sense grazed livestock on such treacherous range and, if they valued their kids as much as their cash-value critters, they warned them not to wander up among the try holes, either. So while he wasn't much more than a spit and a holler from Black Hawk, it felt as if he and whatever was haunting the nape of his neck had the now halfway-healed slope all to themselves.

The survey map might or might not have been more accurate than his rough copy of the patch Elroy Garner's claim number had to be on, some damned where around here. There was more than one old try hole, their edges softened by the ferocious mountain climate, and even the spoil piles reclaimed by weeds this late in the game. Fireweed, chickweed, and the plantain the Indians called "white man's footprints" waved Longarm over to try holes he might otherwise have missed, and he had to try eight of them before he found the right one, where things had gone dreadfully wrong.

As Longarm put it together, Elroy Garner hadn't sunk the shaft near the top of the rise. He'd just noticed how the earlier prospectors, widening their holes for elbow room as they followed softer blossom rock into the mountain at a thirty-odd-degree angle, had blasted out and abandoned a lot of rock the color of wet blackboard slate, only harder. Longarm knew only a chemical assay could tell him whether it was telluride or not. But it looked more like the tough-to-refine but sometimes rich ore than any other rock in these parts, so, like Mattie Garner's man had done the night she'd thought he ran off with Kerry Rose, Longarm gingerly eased himself down the muddy slope into the long-abandoned hole in the ground. The daylight from the adit behind him offered just enough illumination to get him to a knee-high barrier of rock that had come down from the untimbered overhang. He knew this was about as far as most kids would have ever explored. But he wasn't a kid, and when he spied an old dust-crusted lantern wedged in a natural wall niche he hauled it out, removed the glass chimney, fiddled some with the old oil wick, and discovered to his dismay that he *could* get the infernal lantern to light. So he cussed it and his own curious nature as, having no excuse to turn back, after all, he leaned his Winchester against the rock barrier and rolled over the same with the lamp held high.

By its flickering light he was able to see the shaft ran about level, now, which wasn't such a great improvement unless one enjoyed striding across mud and batshit to where an even bigger barrier of fallen rock barred all further progress. He was about to turn back when he swung the lantern back for a closer look at what might have been a dead and dried-up bat, if this had been just another abandoned try hole. But a human hand was a human hand, even gnawed by rats and shriveled to little more than black tendons holding fried-bacon colored bones together and, unless Longarm wanted to assume that one hand sticking out of the dark gray rock pile had crawled down here all by itself, he had to assume there was somebody attached to the wrist that went with those disgusting five fingers.

There was. It took Longarm more time and stomach churnings than he'd have chosen to dig the long-dead rascal out enough to matter. For Longarm had to move each rock he removed from the pile with considerable caution, with one ear cocked for the glassy tinkle of more mountain fixing to come down on both of them. But he was able to follow the outstretched skeletal arm, encased in the mud-starched sleeve of its work shirt, to where the caved-in skull stared hollow-eyed at him with some of its hair still clinging to it, in case that was all the I.D. the damned fool had been packing when he'd gone down a try hole alone, like some lawmen Longarm could mention.

But in the end there was a wallet in the hip pocket of the dead man's bib overalls and, while ground water hadn't done wonders for either the leather or paper, Longarm was satisfied he'd found poor Mattie's missing husband, unless some other damned fool had managed to bury himself alive with Elroy Garner's voter registration and mine union card on him.

Hanging on to the documentary evidence, Longarm gingerly covered the remains with some of the smaller rocks he'd shifted the other way, muttering, "You just lie still here 'til we can get your widow a good lawyer to protect this claim I'd say you both suffered some to earn. She's going to have to have that divorce set aside before she puts in for this gloomy but hopefully profitable estate of yours, Elroy. I doubt she'll have much trouble taking her bitch against you back. Anyone can see you didn't have Kerry Rose with you down here when you somehow managed to kill your fool self."

Having made sure no fool kids would stumble over the remains before they could be removed from the mountain properly, Longarm headed back to the adit. It was just as well he hadn't had to go any deeper into the mountain. For the little coal oil left in the old lantern gave out halfway there. But since he could see the bitty blue square of sky up yonder now, he just tossed the useless lantern aside and trudged on up, his Winchester at port until, emerging from the earth again, he saw nobody laying for him in the late-afternoon silence of the secluded dell.

By the time he'd topped the lower rise between the dead man's claim and the town his poor young widow still worked in, Longarm had really started wondering why he felt so sure, despite all evidence to the contrary, that some damned body was keeping an eye on him, if not a gun muzzle, from somewhere among the haunted rises all around.

He saw his pony tethered lonesome far below. There wasn't anyone on the road down yonder, either way. He still spun around, a round in the chamber of his carbine, to spy nothing coming down the slope behind him, after all. The pony seemed happy to see him, or more likely anxious to get back to water and oats in town. But that was only fair, so as Longarm mounted up he told it, "I don't think we'd best tell Mattie, personal, what we just found out here. She cries a heap about her missing man, even after a good screwing and, once she knows what a poor excuse she's been using for the same, I just don't want to be there. Lawyers are paid to break news like that for a modest cut of the dinero they wrangle out of probate court for you. Some son of a bitch may as well earn his fee."

The barb didn't have to answer. Critters had no need for delicate feeling about anyone they'd screwed unless they were fixing to screw them some more.

Longarm smoked down a cheroot as he rode along, riding wide of the stretch he'd been ambushed on that time by cutting up over a hogback, and pretended not to notice when, coming down out of the sunset sky into town at an unusual angle, he spied a couple screwing on a picnic blanket in a grassy draw. They pretended not to notice him, either, if they did. They were going at it hot and heavy as he swung around the first outcrop he could get to without busting into an obvious and likely embarrassing full gallop.

As he rode on down among the miners' shacks that likely afforded less romantic fornication, he thought back to what that fat girl at the courthouse had said about going for picnics in the surrounding hills with gents who didn't appreciate her. That hadn't been her, back here. He wondered just where the poor chubby little thing might be right now, and whether she'd appreciate a good humping half as much as that other gal he'd just caught at it seemed to. He wondered why he was wondering such a dumb thing. He told his pony, "Billy Vail never sent me all the way up here to get laid and, if I did just have to get laid, I've made better-looking friends by far in these parts, hear?"

But as lights down below began to wink on against the coming nightfall, Longarm knew that, strictly speaking, that just wasn't true. He knew it would be best for old Mattie if she didn't see any recent lovers for a spell, and as for the no-longer-young but still mighty frisky Chinese widow, there was now the distinct possibility that he'd have to arrest her, and he was already in enough trouble if things panned out grim as that!

He'd meant what he'd told Squire Tierney about high-grading and, as far as he knew, the Hong Lee Mao clan hadn't been up to anything worse. On the other hand, Sweet William and that wicked Barbara Allan had to be holed up with some other crooks. If one assumed that gang of Union Irishmen weren't sheltering the outlaw pair from the south, there was at least an even chance Sweet William was in with a rival gang and . . .

"We could be playing chess when the name of the game is just old-fashioned checkers," he warned his pony or, in point of fact, himself. "We'd best put you in the livery and me in the hotel across the street, and then we'd best just sit tight and give some of the flies we've stirred up time to settle. For it's tough to catch flies in the dark, even when they ain't buzzing every which way."

Keeping the promise he'd made to himself and his horse, Longarm turned in right after an All-American supper of venison steak, home fries and blackberry pie, cooked by a colored man at the Greek joint near the Blossom Rock Hotel. Then he went upstairs with the *Rocky Mountain News* and a couple of magazines to see how it felt to get a good night's sleep after a sensible turn-in.

It was going on nine-thirty, and he'd just discovered to his disgust that the otherwise swell yarn he'd been reading was an infernal old *serial*, when he heard someone rapping gently on his chamber door.

It sounded more like a female than a raven. But he still hauled his .44-40 out of the holster he'd hung over the bedpost as he rose in his stocking feet, pants, and undershirt to pad silently to the door and demand, "*Quien est?*"

"Please, Deputy Long, I don't want anyone else to know about this visit!" his mysterious visitor replied, in a nervous as well as female tone.

Knowing it was neither Mattie nor the Oriental

126

widow, and hoping that fat girl looked better in the dark, Longarm answered, *"Si, si un momento,"* and doused the one lamp on his side of the door before opening it.

She was naturally illuminated from behind by the hall lamps. That had been the general idea. She was too skinny to be that fat girl from the courthouse. She was all alone, as well. So he hauled her inside with his free hand, shoved her against the door as he shut it, and patted her down for anything firmer than breasts as she gasped, "What's the matter? What have I done? Why are you talking to me so Spanish?"

He led her over to the bed and sat her on it as he reached for a match, saying, "So far you ain't done nothing and that's the way I aim to keep it. I didn't realize I was speaking Spanish until you mentioned it. But the last time a situation like this came up there was a pack of bandidos trying to bust through my door with a sweet and tempting señorita."

He struck a light. As he lit the lamp on the bed table he saw it was the young whore from Squire Tierney's Peerless Saloon, the ugly one in the sleazy red and black dress. He said, "Well, whatever you are you don't look Mexican. Is it safe to assume Squire Tierney sent you over with a message for me?"

She shook her head, her hair being stove-polish black and stiff as if she'd painted it as well, and told him, "The boss doesn't know I'm here. Before I go on, do I have your word you won't tell him about this visit, honey?"

He growled, "It depends on the reason for this unexpected honor and, by the way, don't be so formal. Call me Deputy Long until I know what this is all about."

She leaned back on her braced elbows as if to give him a better view of her chest. Her breasts were about all she had going for her and he was sure she knew it. But when he just went on staring down at her, like a wooden Indian, with his gun down at his side but still in hand, she said, "Barbie told me you were stronger willed than most men. I can't say I'm used to having a man look at me as if I was a bug on a pin. I know I don't like it. But now I see why she was afraid to come her ownself."

He doubted she had enough of a reach to present any danger to him from where he'd set her. So he put his .44-40 back where he'd hung it earlier and demanded, "Get to the point. Who sent you, about what?"

To which she coyly replied in a little singsong voice, off key:

> "In Scarlet Town where I was bound
> There was a fair maid dwelling
> And every lad said well-away
> To fickle Barbara Allan!"

He nodded and said, "I follow your drift. What's her deal?"

So the poor little drab tried, "If she was willing to stand and deliver the bigger prize you're after, do you reckon you could find it in your heart to forgive some of her, ah, naughty little pranks in the dead and forgotten past?"

Longarm didn't think this would be the time to point out that Dave Rice, Proddy Bob Trevor, and at least one member of a stagecoach crew were dead but hardly forgotten, thanks to what she dismissed as little pranks. So he just asked who she was and, more important, what she was to Barbara Allan, and whether she was authorized to deal or just sniff about for possible scraps.

The skinny whore allowed she was most often called

Slats Sullivan, and identified Barbara Allan as a sister in sin who'd *really* gone wrong, explaining, "It's not wise for businesswomen like me to fall for a customer. Most of us fell into the business as the result of betrayal by a false-hearted man to begin with. If men were any damned good, damned few of us would be able to make a living off the fickle fuckers."

Longarm picked up his shirt and fished out a smoke as he told her not to be bitter and stick to the fucking point. So she said, "All right, my old chum was making a good living off the renting of her rump when this sweet-talking outlaw put a bug in her ear as well. He convinced her the two of them could make way more money working together than either could apart. She already knew what fools men were about a woman who wasn't downright hideous being willing to smile at them when they deserved to be slapped. So with her acting as the bait or sometimes just the lookout—"

"I know how they were working together," he cut in. "I got an almost thirty-page dossier on Sweet William and Barbara Allan and, by the way, is her name really Barbara?"

Slats looked disgusted and replied, "Surely you jest. Did you think my poor old mother really named her sweet little baby Slats? Never mind what anyone's real name might be. She sent me to tell you she's grown mighty weary of the owlhoot trail and to ask you whether you think she could clear herself with the law by handing over the killer you're really after."

He lit the cheroot in a contemplative manner and shook out the match thoughtfully before he replied, "What I think may or may not jibe with the thoughts of my superiors. Marshal Vail can be such an old fuss about premeditated murder. But before I commit my ownself to any sort of a deal, I'd like to read the fine print. Is fickle Barbara Allan just out to sell me the present whereabouts of her lover-boy and let me do all the work, or might she be willing to really sell him to me, say, asleep in bed with his guns out of reach?"

Slats said, "I could ask. What would be in it for her if she gave him to you already stuffed, say, with knock-out drops and lead?"

He blew smoke out both nostrils and muttered, "Sounds like the gal of every man's dreams, if one counts nightmares. The fliers out on Sweet William do read dead or alive. So the petty details don't matter, as far as her just wanting to get rid of him. But to tell the truth, I just can't savvy why she'd want to go to so much trouble, just to rid herself of a pest."

Slats blinked at him and protested, "She *has* to get rid of him if she wants to go back to being an honest whore, don't she?"

To which he replied with a shake of his head, "She *was* rid of him, less than a full week ago, when the law picked him up in Arnold Wells. We have yellow sheets on him reaching all the way back to Clay County, Missouri, and he's been eligible for a hanging since before he was old enough to vote. Yet she murdered two deputies to get him out of jail up yonder when all she'd have needed to do was pure nothing."

Slats still looked stupid as ever, so he blew more annoyed smoke and started to point out that the other dumb bitch was only known to the law as a name, and a fake one at that. But then he wondered if anyone could be as dumb as he'd be, explaining the obvious when they just might think he was even dumber than those deputies in Arnold Wells. So he only said, lamely, "I reckon she figured he'd turn her in, as well, if she didn't help him get away, huh?"

Slats still looked mighty puzzled. He asked, "Didn't

she tell you about busting Sweet William out of jail just before they came back here to their old stamping grounds?"

Slats looked sincere as she replied, "She never even told me his name was Sweet William. I thought it was Jake. Do you want him or not?"

Longarm nodded grimly and said, "I want him." And if he failed to say he wanted both of them, what the hell, there seemed to be a heap of fibbing going on around here in any case.

Slats nodded and said, "All right. I'll tell her you said you'd rather have him delivered unconscious or worse with no needless gunplay. I'll get back to you when and if she tells me how she figures to handle her end of the bargain and— We do have a bargain, don't we?"

Longarm knew he'd hate himself in the morning, but he nodded soberly that night and Slats said she'd try and get back to him this side of midnight. So he let her out and, as soon as he heard the last of her heels clicks on the stairs, he put on his boots, duds, and six-gun before making certain he had sixteen rounds in his Winchester's magazine. For whether poor old ugly Slats knew it or not, fickle Barbara Allan or just as likely the murderous sidewinder she slithered with were out to set somebody up indeed, and how many gals busted men out of jail just so they could turn him over to the law?

It took until a heap closer to midnight than Longarm enjoyed up a dark alley. So when Slats Sullivan finally returned, alone, his voice was downright growly when he stopped her from opening the side door of his hotel by announcing, "Over here, Slats!" from behind the ashcans he was forted-up behind at the dead end of the alley.

Her ugly face was a barely visible blur in the darkness as she groped her way toward him asking, "What's going on? Why didn't you wait for me up in your room, honey?"

He hauled her behind the lined-up ashcans with him, growling, "I can't wait to see whose honey I might be. It's a good thing they give plenty of hot water at the Blossom Rock. For nothing stops bullets and buckshot better than coal ash and, as you can see now, we have anyone coming at us with a Le Mat outlined swell against the light from the street lamps out front."

She laughed incredulously and asked, "Did you think I'd be dumb enough to lead an armed attack on a man of your rep? I'm only willing to *sell* my ass, honey. I'm not about to get it blown off in a crossfire setup!"

He chuckled at the imaginary picture and said, "All right, let's get to the ambush they asked you to lead me into, then."

She stared up at him, slack jawed, to protest, "You're as mad as the mad dog Barbie's only trying to get shed of, damn it! What call have you to suspect me of anything but fair screwing and good will? I'm only an innocent go-between and I'm already sorry I ever let Barbie drag me into her troubles this damned far! We both know you'd know who *I* was and where to find me if you survived any damned trap I tried to lead you into. Do you really think I'd be that dumb, knowing how Joe and Kevin made out when *they* set out to back-shoot you?"

Longarm moved her around him into the niche formed by the ashcans and a corner of the bricked-in blind alley as he smiled thinly and said, "Let's talk about that. Your boss, Squire Tierney, told me those old boys were working on their own as sore losers. Might he have told you to tell me a tale about Sweet William

132

and Barbara Allan, hoping I'd come up yet another blind alley, wagging my tail behind me?"

She assured him, "You're crazy, honey. My boss knows nothing about this deal. Barbie asked me not to even tell him she was back in town before she got her outlaw boyfriend off her back!"

He cradled the Winchester more politely across his arms, yet sounded no less reserved as he told her, "I don't doubt she's used to holding out on menfolk, Slats. But lest we both spend the whole damned night here, catching our deaths in this star-frosted air, suppose you tell me what you were sent to tell me, on your sweet innocent lonesome?"

She said, "I swear nobody followed me here. I'd have got back sooner if I hadn't had to, ah, entertain a few big spenders. I told Barbie what you said about wanting to take the pest alive. She says she don't care how you take him, as long as you don't expect her to wind up dead. She suspects he's already suspicious of her intent. It was her notion and none of his own to come back here to Central City after things got too hot for 'em in other parts. She's got him holed up out of sight, of course, and she's been the one going out to fetch food and buy all the newspapers lest they miss something about all you lawmen hunting 'em. It's always easier for a woman to appear in public with her hair and face paint different. But he can't seem to understand her staying out on the town while he's holed up so tight."

Longarm nodded soberly and said, "Men with jealous streaks ought to consider the pasts of their women before they plan any futures with 'em. In sum, you're saying he's been cramping her plans for her own future with his demanding ways. Get to the good part. How do

133

you gals figure I'd best take him without any help from either of you?"

Slats said, "Oh, she said it was all right with her if I just told you where the man you're after ought to be, asleep, alone, about now. I hope you won't be sore, honey, but I did tell her you seemed sort of reluctant to pardon her entire, and so she said it might be best if she just sort of fed you the rascal incognito. Her new plan calls for me to lead you to the shanty they've been holed up in all this time, then leave the rest of it up to you. You ought not to have time to hunt down Barbie once you have Sweet William to take in alive, right?"

He mulled her words over a spell before he decided, "I don't like it, much. But when the mountain won't come to Mohammed we'd best get it on up the road."

Chapter 10

It was farther than he'd expected and more up the slope than any road or even cinder patch worth mention. The skinny whore had a good sense of direction in the dark, considering how she kept insisting she'd only been to the shanty in question a couple of years back, before her sister in sin had ridden off along a more primrose path as the infamous Barbara Allan

By the time they'd made their way over considerable hill and dale in the almost total darkness, Longarm had gotten a few more details out of Slats, albeit nothing that might lead him directly to anyone but Sweet William. She assured him she knew little or nothing about him, let alone any connection he might have with the James and Younger gang. She insisted she'd heard nothing about any jailbreak just before the deadly duo had returned to Gilpin County. So he couldn't pursue the odd reasoning of any gal who'd shoot it out with the law to get her man away from the same, only to turn him into it a few days and not all that many miles later. It made more sense to ask how the fugitive couple had settled on just where to hole up once they got back here.

Slats said, "Oh, that's easy. I doubt he knew about it. But she sure did. You see, there was this one old mining man who dwelt alone in a shanty of his own construction, out of town a ways, and Barbie got to know him well indeed because he was sort of shy about showing his face around the Peerless. I reckon he feared others would accuse him of being a randy old goat, see?"

Longarm grimaced and said, "I'm commencing to. They both sound mighty fastidious. I take it the old geezer ain't living at the same address these days?"

She giggled in a cruel-hearted way and explained, "He's not living anywhere. She came up the hill one evening to make him come and found him gone. The doc said it was a heart attack. Barbie said he'd died owing her a heap of money for services rendered and nobody argued when she put in a claim for his modest property. That's how come I know the way. She brought me up this way more than once to show it off to me. We were sort of planning to fix it up and, well, start our own business far from the crowd. But then she took up with this good-looking but otherwise useless road agent and the rest you know."

Longarm said, "The hell you say. Where in thunder *is* the damned shanty you keep talking about?"

She paused on the gritty slope just above him to peer about for her bearings. Then she said, "Oops, I fear we've overshot it in the dark. That lighter patch of black down that way looks as if it might be old Smitty's tin roof."

Longarm stared the same way until, sure enough, he could barely make out the mass of an apparently isolated hillside shanty. He asked which side the door was on. She told him, "Downslope. This is where we part company, honey. I'll be down at the Peerless if you'd like to drop by later and let me know who won."

He chuckled fondly and hunkered down to lay his Winchester on the uphill side of them before he pulled her down beside him. She didn't resist all that much, but protested, "You sure pick funny times and places, honey. But, all right, as along as I can get on top, and you will use a rubber, won't you?"

He didn't answer until he'd unclipped the handcuffs from the back of his gun rig and snapped one loop around her right wrist. Then, as he cuffed her wrist to her left ankle before she knew what he was really up to, he told her, "I won't keep you in suspense that long, Slats. You just stay put, right here, and I'll be back directly to either set you forever free or arrest you for attempted murder, depending."

Then he rose again, Winchester in hand, to warn her as she commenced to cry, "Keep it down to a dull roar. Let him guess I'm coming if he hasn't already been told." Then he started easing down toward the dark shanty, digging his heels into the bare grit lest he arrive on his ass by express. Halfway down he glanced back. He could just make out her crouched form as she struggled in total silence to rise, without much luck. He muttered, "Good girl. Smart girl, leastways," and kept moving down in the darkness until he was able to flatten one ear against the rough cedar siding. The shack was silent as a tomb. He eased himself along the vertical planks, ducking under a small window he had to get past on that wall. He paused with a silent curse and let his heart beat fifty times before he eased on after some infernal busted glass crunched under his boot heel in the damned dark. He froze again when he heard other

137

movement by something or someone unseen in the blackness all around. He didn't hear it again. He had no notion what he'd heard. Neither mice nor men made all that distinct a sound when they were trying to pussy-foot. It could have been no more than old sun-dried planking snapping back in place in the damper night air. Old houses seemed to creak as if with minds of their own.

Then he got to where the door was supposed to be and felt his belly roll over inside him as his cautiously questing left hand felt nothing but empty air where door paneling should have been. The damned door had been swung open in the dark and, yep, that had likely been the sound he'd just heard. So the only question before the house was the exact location of the *other* keen-eared son of a bitch!

Longarm glanced up at the starry sky above. With no moon up yonder, not even the Milky Way lit the slopes all about enough to matter. It'd still be suicide trying to enter a jet-black room or more with any light at all at one's back, if anyone was inside, on the prod. On the other hand, putting himself in the other rascal's boots, Longarm wondered if he'd want to box himself in a wooden shack with no other exit. Then, knowing how disgusting that sounded to him he opted for a crouching continuation of his trip around the outside of the house and just got back to the uphill side when he heard all hell bust loose between him and where he'd left old Slats on her skinny ass up yonder. He fired his Winchester upslope, from the hip, at the dark figure outlined by its own muzzle flashes. Once he'd done that things got mighty quiet where he was, albeit dogs barked, doors and windows popped open and so forth, as shanty town woke up again to demand some answers to that late-night din.

Knowing he'd have to answer to the local law as well, Longarm struck a match and gagged, "Aw, shit!" as he saw what lay sprawled on the slope at his feet.

The male figure lay facedown atop what was left of old Slats, with the hole Longarm had blown in the back of his white shirt still welling red ruin, and a smoking Le Mat gripped in each dead or dying fist.

First things coming first, Longarm shook out the match and rolled the limp bastard off the limp whore before he struck another light. He didn't really need to feel the side of her throat for a pulse. He'd never yet seen anyone go on pulsing after getting their face blown half off by number-nine buck, and the other holes blown in her couldn't have done her much good, either.

Propping his Winchester on the man's body lest he grit up the acton, Longarm quickly uncuffed the dead girl's wrist from her ankle as he told her, "I've got enough questions to answer and I'm sure sorry about all this, whether you were out to set me up or vice versa."

He composed her limbs and pulled her skirts down for her before turning his attention back to the rascal he'd shot, too late to do Slats much good. By flickering matchlight the young face staring blankly up at him with a shy little smile on its pale lips looked close enough to that blurry old tintype of Sweet William and one of the Ford boys. Longarm took the big and still warm Le Mats from the cadaver's dead hands before they could freeze to the grips. Both shotgun barrels had been discharged into poor old Slats, and there were only two rounds left in one cylinder. Longarm told the now much calmer looking cuss, "You couldn't figure what that was up ahead of you in the dark. The last thing you were expecting was a gal in a print dress, rolled up in a sort of ball and likely moving as odd as she must have sounded to you in the dark. So you just done what comes natural to a trigger-happy asshole, and had I known you were almost out of ammunition you'd be in better shape right now to answer me. I sure wish you could, Sweet William. For I still have lots of questions, starting with whether it was you or me someone wanted too dead to compare notes!"

Nobody important fussed at Longarm as half the town, it seemed, gathered up the slope with lanterns and torches enough to light up the scene considerable. Sheriff Hiram Blake showed up, looking untidy and sleepy headed, just about the time Longarm had the situation sorted out with the county lawmen who'd gotten there earlier. So Longarm explained to Blake, "Sweet William killed the whore and I killed him. I just told your boys I'd be proud to help the county with its paperwork. I got some paperwork of my own to turn in and so, for openers, I'm going to want both bodies tidied up and photographed. I'll want depositions from anyone who can I.D. either of them for certain, as well."

Sheriff Blake rubbed his head some more with the palm of his hand as he yawned and said, "There's no mystery about the dead female. Even though there's barely enough left of her face to photograph, there must be a hundred men on this hill right now who've had her three ways for two dollars. How come the other stiff killed her?"

Longarm said, "I'm still working on that. She led me up here to capture him, she said. He might have shot her in the dark by mistake or he might have known exactly who he was shooting at. Some men take it serious when a whore tries to take advantage of them. They don't seem to know the rules of the game."

Blake muttered, "Old Slats should have known better

140

than to mess with such lethal gents. But nobody ever accused her of being bright."

Then he called out, "Slade and Perkins, front and center! I want both these bodies carried down to the morgue, now. Deputize some help if you can't get a buckboard up here. But get 'em both down, poco tiempo!"

Longarm had meanwhile tucked both the dead man's massive Le Mat revolvers in his own waistband, under his coat, and turned to head back down the slope himself. Blake tagged along until Longarm turned in at that old shanty. When Blake asked why, Longarm said, "You go on back to town and your bed if you've a mind to, Sheriff. When a man boils out of a hidey-hole at me with a Le Mat in each hand I sort of like to explore it some."

He didn't really want Blake's company as he struck yet another match and entered the old shanty to light the first oil lamp he came to, hanging on a chain above a rickety table in the center of the one room. But it was Blake's county, and so he had to be polite when the sheriff pried open a stove lid and commenced to poke up the banked coal fire in the corner kitchen range, muttering, "If this is coffee in this mighty cold tin pot here, I might just wake up, after all. What else are we looking for here, Longarm?"

The younger and much more alert lawman placed his carbine on the table and stared thoughtfully around, replying, "Won't know before I see it," as his wide-set gray eyes took in the rumpled bed in another corner and the pasteboard boxes of fresh supplies near the stove old Blake was messing with. He asked if that was a new can of Arbuckle coffee or an old empty one on the pine shelf just above the pot. Blake reached out, shook it, and declared, "Half full. Smells fresh. What of it?"

141

To which Longarm could only reply, "Slats told me true about this place. Part way, at least. She said Sweet William and his no-shit fickle Barbara Allan came back here to Central City because she knew of this old semi-isolated shanty, and knew nobody lived here anymore."

Blake shrugged and said, "I could have told you that. The place has been for sale a spell. Nobody with a lick of sense would bid on it, of course. Every once in a while Kerry Rose writes to find out whether the place has been sold or not."

Longarm gasped in surprise and demanded, "Kerry Rose, that other whore everyone thought Elroy Garner was messing with, is the owner of record here?"

Blake lifted the lid of the coffeepot to mutter, "Come on, damn it, *boil*! I'm missing something, Longarm. Everyone in town knows old Silent Smith, or Smitty, left this old shack to Kerry Rose, the blow job of his dreams. Only she's been over to Steamboat Springs for some time and, while the bank's been trying to sell this modest plot and crackerbox for her, nobody's even seen fit to walk this damned far up the slope for a look-see. It seems mighty obvious to me that Sweet William and his doxie knew the place was empty, needed a place to hide out, and there you go. What's so mysterious about it?"

Longarm said, "Where Barbara Allan might be, herself, for openers. She sent her pal, Slats, to lead me to her unwanted outlaw lover-boy. There's not much mystery left about that. She just got rid of both her lover-boy and the only witness to the deal who could point her out for certain. I don't see how she could have planned things quite so neat. It's as likely she just counted on poor Slats being discreet."

Blake was starting to wake up now, despite the refusal of the coffeepot to perk. He still yawned, however, before he said, "They might have had one of them lizzy-gal friendships going. Some say whores don't fall for men half as hard as they can fall for one another, lizzy-gal style. Some say old Kerry Rose went in for that, too. Lord knows there wasn't anything she wouldn't do with her sassy mouth for a man. It's too bad she don't work for Squire Tierney no more. If Kerry Rose was still in town, she might be able to put you on to any other gal old Slats liked all that well, that way."

Longarm snapped his fingers and said, "I'd just as well we're not queer, Sheriff. For if we were I'd likely kiss you right now. Don't you see how it's starting to fall together, you smart cuss?"

Blake said he didn't recall saying anything all that smart. So Longarm told him, "William or maybe Jake Allan picked up his Barbara Allan somewhere out here in the farther west, after he got out here. That would have been just about the time Kerry Rose, the otherwise disgusting but beautiful bawd who'd do anything for a buck announced she'd come into money of her own and meant to open her own house in Steamboat Springs!"

Blake said, "She did. Some of the boys have been over there and they say it's about the best parlor house in Colorado. You surely don't think the mysterious Barbara Allan and the infamous Kerry Rose could be one and the same!"

Longarm rummaged for something to go with their coffee as the pot commenced to perk on the stove at last. But as he did so he said, half to himself, "It has a few holes in it, I'll allow, but it explains more than it leaves out. Would you even consider hiding out in an empty shanty unless you knew for certain it would stay empty all the time you were there?"

143

Blake started to say something dumb. Then he nodded soberly and replied, "I follow your drift. Nobody but the owner of the property could say for sure whether anyone was likely to show up or not. But damn it, Longarm, Kerry Rose has always been a whore, not a bandit queen like that Belle Starr back east in the Indian Nation."

Longarm smiled thinly and replied, "You'd be surprised what they call Belle Starr around Fort Smith. Try her this way. Say we're both right. Say an impulsive gal with a love of novelty took up with a more exciting customer than usual who robbed banks and stagecoaches, and say they made enough at it for her to buy her own whorehouse. Everyone I've talked to about Kerry Rose agrees she was devoted to her job, and it's only natural to want one's own business when one's good at a trade. Say she pulled a few more jobs with him, whether she wanted to or not, after getting things set up pretty good for her, at least, over in Steamboat Springs. Then say she began to weary of those extra shifts along the owlhoot trail and decided she'd best get rid of a lover-boy she'd tired of."

Blake rummaged two china mugs out of a cupboard for them as he replied, "Nobody ever accused Kerry Rose of consistency to one dong. I recall the night she encouraged our volunteer firemen to win a ballgame against Lawson by taking on all nine of 'em and, some say, their firehouse dalmation as well. But hold on. You told me when you first got here that she or some damned doxie, at least, had just busted Sweet William out of jail, blowing away two lawmen in the process!"

As Blake poured, Longarm grumbled, "That's one loose end I'll allow I'm having trouble with. There's an outside chance she feared he'd sell her to us to save his own neck. She knew he knew we wanted her as well as him for gunning at least one shotgun messenger. She knew without him having to tell her that a man who'd hang to protect even a decent gal, when offered a chance to turn state's evidence, is a rarity indeed. So let's say she only sprung him in order to make sure he could never talk and . . . shit, that's dumb as soon as you say it, ain't it?"

Blake picked up his cup, tasted experimentally, and said with a sigh, "Well, it's coffee, I suspect. I agree not even a fickle-hearted female would go to all that much trouble just to shut one lover-boy up. She could have just shot him dead in the Arnold Wells jail and let the whole thing be written off as a bungled escape attempt, right?"

Longarm muttered, "I just said that. She didn't just bust Sweet William out. She busted him out so slick we still can't say how she done it. I doubt Kerry Rose will tell me, whether she's really Barbara Allan or not. But I got me some telegrams to send and some train connections to make if I mean to get over to Steamboat Springs this side of breakfast."

Blake's jaw dropped. He told Longarm flatly, "You could likely make it up to Routt County in that time aboard a flying carpet outa an Arab fairy tale. There just ain't no way you're going to get there this side of late tomorrow afternoon by railroad, let alone on horseback, Longarm. We're talking the far side of the Continental Divide and across the Upper Colorado. There being no possible way to lay tracks along such a bumpy route, nobody's ever even tried! Aside from which, if Kerry Rose is Barbara Allan, how do you expect to find her up in Steamboat Springs when you get there?"

Longarm put down his cup and picked up his Winchester, saying, "I won't, if the two gals are one and the same. That's my point in heading out right now. For there's only one late-night narrow gauge that'll carry either of us anywhere near Steamboat Springs, and we're sure to notice one another if we both make the same run aboard it."

Chapter 11

In the end Longarm had breakfast aboard the narrow gauge and didn't get off at Steamboat Springs with his saddle and such until well after ten A.M. But at least he felt sure, for the railroad conductor agreed, there was no way in hell anyone could have beaten him up to the northwest corner of the infernal state by any faster means of transportation. The damned tangle of transfer points he'd just chased all over the damned Rocky Mountains was simply the shortest way there was or would be until they drove that broad-gauge line they kept promising through Steamboat Springs.

No steamboat had ever navigated the hot headwaters of the Yampa River where they boiled out of the rumbling guts of the continent at well over six thousand feet above sea level. The results had simply reminded the mountain men who'd found the fool springs of the way steamboats churned and puffed away. The town itself served as the county seat and business center for the surrounding high country. They raised more livestock and some said hell in Routt County than anything else. It was up to the state government, rather than Billy Vail or Longarm, to inquire as to where so many cows could have come from, so far out in the middle of nowhere. It seemed obvious a lot of money could be made raising stock that way, once Longarm stuck his saddle and possibles in the livery tack room across from the track-side loading chutes, and discovered upon asking that they charged more than two bits a day for the hire of even a busted-down riding mule.

He slipped the breed stablehand a nickel to watch over his belongings, anyway, and allowed that with luck he might not have to hire a mount or even a room. He'd told everyone to wire him in care of the Steamboat Springs Western Union, so that was where he headed next to discover that, sure enough, telegrams could beat trains over the Continental Divide easy as pie.

Sheriff Blake had wired that the bodies had been not only photographed but put on public display in front of the morgue. So Blake was pleased to inform Longarm that the gent he'd downed just a mite late for Slats Sullivan's good had been identified as indeed the Le Mat—wielding son of a bitch who'd stopped the mail stage and various wayfaring innocents who'd neither forgotten nor forgiven him. Blake added they'd had to get poor Slats below ground a lot sooner because of the way her torn-up head and busted-open torso had attracted flies, despite all the naptha they'd sprayed over both the bodies. Blake added the photographs would be mailed to Longarm's Denver office as per his request.

There was a wire sent later but naturally waiting up here with other messages, and this one was from that lawyer one of Blake's deputies said he was related to by marriage. He just assured Longarm tersely that he'd look into the matter of the Garner mining claim and that he agreed a divorce on grounds of desertion only counted when and if there'd been a true desertion. Longarm started to write down the lawyer's name and office address in Central City and decided he'd just as soon not know how things turned out. He'd done his best for old Mattie, considering nobody had asked him.

The wire from Billy Vail of course complained he'd *Deleted by Western Union* done the job he'd been sent to do and demanded to know what he thought he was apt to accomplish in Steamboat Springs. In Billy Vail's view, Sweet William had been the prize and, while the doxie who'd betrayed him had no doubt murdered some local repeat *local* lawmen, there was no getting around the fact that she and her unfortunate sister in sin had set the more hangable outlaw up and that ergo no judge and jury was apt to give her enough time at hard labor to justify the time and trouble of tracking her down, let alone the long tedious trial that was bound to follow.

Longarm tossed Vail's order to get his *Deleted by Western Union* home in the wastebasket and picked up yellow blank and pencil to block-letter his own reasons for tracking Barbara Allan to the bitter end. Then he balled that up and tossed it in the wastebasket as well. For he knew it would only rile old Billy to be told, however politely, he was an asshole.

Having finished for now at Western Union, Longarm strode over to the nearby courthouse to pay at least a courtesy call on Sheriff Blake's opposite number in this county. As it turned out, their full-time sheriff was off in the hills hunting a stock-killing grizzly with most of the men and boys in Steamboat Springs. The deputy left in charge wrote down Longarm's name and said it was all right with him if Longarm wanted to nose about on federal matters. He added, "Adopting stray cows lest they starve up among the green glades of the park range ain't a federal crime, since last I looked it up. So might I ask, in case anybody cares, just who you might be after up here, about what?"

Longarm told him as he fed them both cheroots and lit them up. The small-town deputy seemed to enjoy a good smoke, cuss his grinning hatchet face, but when Longarm got around to his suspicions about their notorious whorehouse madam, the deputy whistled softly and said, "I don't see how you're ever going to get out of here alive with Kerry Rose, Uncle Sam. Aside from running the best whorehouse this side of Denver, she has a sort of personal following, if you follow my drift."

Longarm nodded and said, "They told me down in Central City that she enjoyed screwing for its own sake. As to whether I'll have to run her in or not, a lot will depend on just where she might have been the last few days, and how good she is at proving it."

As Longarm turned to go, the local lawman rose from behind his desk to call out, "Hold on, now, damn it. The sheriff told me to try and keep the peace while he tracked down that disorderly bear. You go busting into Kerry Rose's place with no more than a hunch to go on and the best thing you can hope for is a quick death. If I was you I'd wait 'til the sheriff and some serious backup rode back from that bear hunt. I just don't have the manpower right now to go up against a serious mob!"

Longarm shrugged and replied, "You ain't me. I've hunted rogue grizzlies. So I know how long it can take and I just haven't that much time to spare."

The deputy pleaded, "Hell, you don't know for certain Kerry Rose had anything to do with your troubles in

Arnold Wells or Gilpin County, damn it!"

To which Longarm soberly replied, "That's why I don't aim to waste more time than I have to. If your Kerry Rose ain't Barbara Allan, then Barbara Allan has to be somebody else, and I don't mean to let her get away."

"How come?" the other lawman demanded, following Longarm out front. "You got her lover-boy, and her chum told you why she was giving him to the law. If she's gone out of the business of highway robbery on her own . . ."

"She owes me, at least, some explanations. You may not care. My boss may not care, but even reformed killers who can turn themselves and anyone else they need to invisible make me nervous as all get out!"

"We heard about her and Sweet William vanishing into thin air with a whole town watching," agreed the local lawman. "There's likely some simple enough explanation, unless you believe in magic. I mean *real* magic."

Longarm said, "I don't. Old Billy's sent me out on some stumpers that *seemed* mighty mystical until I figured out how it was done. So far I've yet to meet up with anyone who could even make a bunny rabbit vanish, fair and square. All those folk over in Arnold Wells were fooled into seeing something happen that couldn't have really happened and, when I catch up with the gal who made it happen, I mean to make her tell me exactly how she done it. Then I mean to make certain she never does it no more. Fickle-hearted women make me nervous, too. It's just dumb to assume anyone who's killed and gotten away with it slick as a whistle may never kill again. The damn fool wearing pants was hardly the most dangerous member of that stickup team, you know. He got picked up like a fool kid in Arnold Wells and blasted away at the wrong target last night in Cen-

151

tral City. I mean to round up the smarter one now."

The county deputy wished him luck but didn't follow. Longarm didn't want to ask on the street for directions to the best whorehouse in the county, and he needed the advice of a gunsmith in any case. So when he spied a big wooden pistol hanging over the plank walk just down the way he went there, next.

The gunsmith in Steamboat Springs was a younger gent of the Hebrew persuasion who agreed with the one in Black Hawk about Le Mat revolvers. When Longarm placed the brace he'd taken from Sweet William on the counter and asked about reloads, the gunsmith shrugged and said, "Reload shmeload, can't you see nobody ever got around to converting either of these antiques? Cap and ball, both of them."

Longarm said, "I noticed that. My question, asking as a federal lawman, is whether you sell the loose powder, shot, and percussion caps a body would need to set these dumb things up to fire."

The gunsmith nodded but said, "For muzzle-loading market guns, yes. Conical rounds, .40 caliber for a Civil War hand cannon, no. If it was a matter of vital importance I'd suggest a few duck-shot in each chamber of the cylinder and a bigger charge, of course, in the bigger barrel below. I'd load and tamp way before I put any caps on the nipples, of course. A thing like a Le Mat going off in your face could take years off your life."

Longarm stared soberly down at the two massive revolvers, musing half to himself, "Last night a mean cuss took years off the life of a fairly young gal with two charges of buck and about fifteen or sixteen conical .44 slugs. If he couldn't have bought such ammo here, might you be able to direct me to a place he might have, here in Steamboat Springs?"

The gunsmith shook his head and sounded as if he meant it when he replied, "Denver, Omaha, maybe. Some bigger town where there may be a market for unusual firearms. Most of my customers prefer .44-40 because they can use the same rounds in both their six-guns and carbines."

Longarm smiled thinly and agreed, "That's what I generally use. You just said why. Is there any natural law saying an old boy couldn't just buy powder, shot, and caps as if for a muzzle loader and then cast his own odd pistol rounds on a good hot kitchen range?"

The gunsmith shrugged and said, "Anything's possible. You want me to sell you some good corned powder and enough loose shot and caps to use it up?"

Longarm started to say no. Then he nodded slowly and replied, "You can peddle me enough to load both these old Le Mats serious, if you'll be kind enough to crimp the caps on the nipples for me. It's been a spell since I last packed a Springfield riflemusket, and I've had accidents with caps now and again, even single shot and aimed straight up, out of doors."

The gunsmith must have wanted his business. As Longarm watched with interest he loaded all eighteen revolving chambers with duck-shot, since that made for neater packing in the smaller spaces, and loaded each 18-gauge barrel with a double charge of deer-crippling *buck*shot, cheerfully pointing out, "Nothing is going to come out of such short barrels with any accuracy, so why not throw a good spread if you have to throw at all?"

Longarm agreed, stuck both Le Mats in his waist band, and began to pay as the gunsmith winced and pleaded, "Listen, let me sell you a nice used two-gun buscadero before you wind up circumcized the way Moses wouldn't want!"

Longarm laughed and didn't argue. He'd once seen the grim results of a gun going off inside a reckless gunslick's pants. He still felt sort of silly, though, even with the tails of his frock coat over the grips of all three guns, as he headed for the whorehouse as the gunsmith had directed him, doubled over with laughter, even after he'd been informed it was a federal matter.

The establishment of Kerry Rose was naturally up a side street on the far side of the tracks from the church and schoolhouse, albeit the town hadn't advanced to possessing a distinct red-light district as yet, and had to settle for just a "wrong side of the tracks" where nice women never went so that their husbands could. Longarm found the corner tobacco shop he'd been directed to look for and there, around the corner, rose the Carpenter's Gothic parlor house of Madam Kerry Rose. The siding was painted a tasteful shade of apple green with tomato-red trim. It could have been worse. It would have looked even wilder with the colors reversed.

Longarm mounted the steps and twisted the brass knob of the door chime. After a time a tough-looking bozo in dire need of a shave and some dental work opened the door a crack to growl, "For Chrissake, it ain't high noon yet, you horny rascal. Try Indian Alice down by the blacksmith's if you're just too proud to jack off."

He would have closed the door had not Longarm shoved a foot in it to growl back, "Open up and let me in. I'm the law." But this served only to inspire more determination on the part of the burly pimp, who not only threw all his own weight against the far side of the door but seemed to be yelling for help. So, lest his poor foot wind up getting mangled, Longarm drew one of the Le Mats, aimed it high lest he mangle someone's head in turn, and blasted a good-sized hole in the door above

the gilt house number. He was surprised by the size of
the hole, the kick of the Le Mat, and the way its throaty
roar echoed up and down the street to bring the neighbors to their own doors and windows. But he must have
surprised the gent on the far side of the door even more.
For it swung on open of its own accord as the vainglor-
ious guardian of the working girl lit out for the back of
the building, if not beyond. So Longarm simply stepped
inside, the smoking Le Mat in hand, and as he heard
cussing and footsteps coming at him in the murky
gloom of a whorehouse closed to the general public, he
decided he might as well draw the other. So he did, just
as a short stubby cuss with a sawed-off scatter-gun hove
into view through a beaded archway down the hallway,
announcing, "Say your prayers and prepare to die, pil-
grim!"

So Longarm fired the other Le Mat's shotgun barrel,
aiming to one side on purpose to rip about a quart of
shattered plaster out of the wall as he peppered the shotgun show-off's shins with duck-shot from the other
hand cannon.

His victim dropped the scatter-gun and fell moaning
to the hall runner, grasping his bleeding shins and demanding someone fetch him his momma and a doctor,
in that order. Then a statuesque nude descended the
stairs in high heels and black mesh stockings with frilly
scarlet garters, demanding some explanation for all this
infernal racket. The hair on her head was as red as her
garters. Her other hair matched her socks. Longarm
ticked the brim of his Stetson to her with the smoking
muzzle of a Le Mat and said, "If you'd be Kerry Rose,
I'd be the law, and I was just explaining to your help
that I'd sure like a word with you."

She came all the way down bold as brass, or at least
aware how seldom a true gent of the old school gunned

a naked female with any looks at all. She caught sight of the tough Longarm had wounded and called Longarm a cocksucker. To which he replied politely, "Takes one to know one, I reckon. He's not hurt too serious. I missed him with my buckshot on purpose. A little tweezer work and a lot of iodine and he'll be good as new, so about our little chat, Madam Rose. . . . "

She called out to someone known as Willie and told her to get her black ass and some hot towels down here directly. Then she turned to Longarm, pointed at a side door off the hall, and said, "In here. I'm, ah, entertaining a visitor in my quarters upstairs."

Longarm didn't mind. He knew she was less likely to have a weapon cached downstairs in the main parlor. So he holstered his two partly emptied Le Mats as he followed her in and across to the corner bar. She got behind the bar, hiding the more shocking two-thirds of her bawdy self from view, but more out of thirst than modesty, it seemed.

As she proceeded to build a brace of heroic morning pick-me-ups on the bar between them, she asked Longarm what else she could do for the law this fine day, adding, "I've taken care of the damned sheriff and the city council, damn it. Who might you be collecting for, the state?"

He shook his head and said, "I'm a federal deputy, ma'am. I ain't interested in your business, and I'd best pass on that lethal-looking drink, this early in the day. Do you have any way of proving where you've been for the past week?"

She sampled one of the tall glasses she'd filled, smacked her lips, and said, "Sure I can, if you're willing to take the word of satisfied customers. This soon after payday I barely get out of bed long enough to make it to the shithouse."

Then she winked lewdly and added, "I wouldn't have it any other way. I just love to fuck, don't you?"

He laughed despite himself and said, "It sure beats herding cows, but there's a time and a place for everything and I'm on serious business right now, if you don't mind."

Then, before she could answer, he heard a movement behind him and spun around, his no-nonsense .44-40 in hand, as a vapidly pretty colored maid in the doorway waved a bloody wet towel at them and announced, "Mistah Spike needs a doc, Miss Rose. His legs is tore up real good."

Kerry Rose nodded, told her to get Doc Keller, and added that she should slide the parlor door shut and see she and her handsome guest were not disturbed. Then, as soon as they were alone again, she told Longarm, "That sofa, yonder in the bay window, just came all the way from Chicago and it's still a virgin, stuck down here in the parlor, poor thing. I don't suppose you'd like to help me christen it?"

"I sure would, if we had the time," he lied gallantly, going on to fill her in on both his recent adventures and the obvious suspicions they led to.

When he got to the part about Sweet William and *some* damned redhead called Barbara Allan using the shanty she still owned in Central City as a hideout, Kerry Rose shrugged her naked shoulders and insisted, "Sticking up stagecoaches doesn't thrill me at all, and as for shooting it out with lawmen for the sake of only one man with one dong, however grand, you have to be joshing. I recall them stopping that mail coach from Winter Park. I was whoring for Squire Tierney in Central City at the time. But this is the first I've heard of anyone called Sweet William or Barbara Allan. Answer me this, handsome: If that treacherous female passenger aboard the stage had been me, how come nobody said so? I just hate to brag, but in my Central City days I was known at least from the neck up to every man for miles around!"

Longarm started to object, couldn't come up with anything to object to, and had to concede, "If you were accused of stealing husbands clean over in Black Hawk your point is well taken, ma'am."

She treated herself to another sip of her evil-looking drink and said with a self-satisfied smirk, "Damned-A. I've been told by more than one admirer I'm just too durned beautiful to be real. Have you ever seen any gal prettier than me in all of Colorado, you uncaring brute?"

He had to admit he hadn't, and he wasn't being gallant. It seemed a crying shame anything so downright sweet and lovely-looking had to be so self-destructive. For he knew Kerry Rose was digging her own early grave with her chosen way of life. Even if she wasn't getting laid much more often than many a happily married gal, the drinking and other bad habits that went with it had to be playing hell with her innards. But since there was only one bad habit he had power to arrest her for, he insisted, "Let's get back to that miner's shack you laid claim to in the gold fields, Madam Rose. Your old chum, Slats Sullivan, got herself killed before we could work out all the nitpicky details. But her other chum, Barbara Allan, wouldn't have hidden her lover-boy there unless she had good reason to feel you weren't fixing to sell the place out from under them, right?"

Kerry Rose nodded thoughtfully and said, "I was wondering why old Slats wrote me that curious letter. I threw it away, so you're going to have to take my word for it unless you can find the letter I wrote back to her."

Longarm made a mental note of that and said, "Let's go along with your memory, for now."

So Kerry Rose told him, "It was a week or so back. Slats wrote that she had a regular who didn't want to be seen in the Peerless by even his minister. So she wanted my permit to shack up with the shy jasper in Smitty's old shack. I wrote back that it was jake with me. For to tell the truth I doubt I'll ever have a buyer for the property at the rate I'm going."

Longarm got out a cheroot—anything had to taste better than the untasted tall one she'd prepared for him —and lit up as he gave himself time to think. Then he decided, "Well, if Slats was acting as a go-between when she led me up there, she could have just as easily lined up the hideout for Barbara Allan. So let's talk about that. If you and the late Slats Sullivan, ah, worked together in Central City long enough to get so chummy, you ought to know who else Slats was chummy with, right?"

Kerry Rose nodded, sipped thoughtfully, and replied, "She didn't have too many chums, male or female. I don't think Slats was ever really cut out to be a good whore. Aside from being sort of ugly she was inclined to argue with men and bitch other women, the poor critter. I didn't mind her dumb remarks about my looks and athletic abilities. I know I'm beautiful, I don't see how anyone could screw better, and like I said, I felt sorry for her."

Longarm nodded soberly and said, "So did I, looking back on it. But we know she was acting for that outlaw pair when she asked your permit to use the old shanty, and we know she was acting for the treacherous Barbara

159

Allan when she led me up there in the end. So what about some Central City lady who wasn't exactly in the same line of business? Say a shop gal or piano player? I know one gal who plays piano in houses of ill repute under the professional name of Red Robin, and she uses henna on her hair as well but, naw, it couldn't have been *her*!"

Kerry Rose sniffed and said, "I don't use henna. I use a coal tar beauty aid all the way from Germany. As to Central City gals who weren't in the life, gals like us just don't socialize with free stuff. Even if we did, I'd recall any chums of Slats who had red hair from any source. I was the only redhead in the bunch, before Slats commenced to emulate me, I mean. The poor thing admired me, you see, despite the mean things she said behind my back. That was why I put up with her. Aren't you thirsty, handsome?"

He blew smoke out of his nostrils and told her, "Not hardly. That stuff may smell like bourbon but it looks more like spinach juice. Anyway, are you saying Slats Sullivan had her *own* hair dyed red on occasion?"

Kerry Rose nodded and explained, "Irish whiskey is hard to come by up here in the hills, so I add just enough creme de menthe to remind me of the auld sod. As to Slats having red hair, of course she had red hair —on her head, at any rate. Didn't you notice when that bastard shot her down right in front of you?"

He tried some of her strong drink. It tasted as awful as he'd expected, but he needed something stronger than tobacco smoke as he swore under his breath and decided, "It works, if one can safely say the late Slats Sullivan wasn't half as well known in Gilpin County as your ownself, Madam Rose."

She dimpled at him to reply, "One safely can. She

160

had only a very few customers, albeit those she had were regulars. You see, she was not only plain but sort of old-fashioned in her approach to fornication. So all she had going for her was a shy way of moving and an unusually tight ring-dang-doo for the moving. Some men seem to like their gals tight, even when they're sort of plain."

Longarm sighed and said, "So much for the hold she had on Sweet William Allan. She as much as told me why she wanted to be shed of him. My own foolishness was occasioned by picturing anything as romantic sounding as a redheaded outlaw gal called Barbara Allan as, well, romantic. Others only described her to me as young and female with no obvious deformities. Some might have even found her decent looking enough to bed down with, since more than one man must have on occasion. It's my own fault for having such good taste, and now I feel dumb as hell."

Kerry Rose suggested, "You'll feel even dumber, later, looking back on this opportunity and wondering why you didn't take me up on it. For if poor old Slats was Barbara Allan, and you gunned her Sweet William just as he was gunning her, I fail to see how you can be on duty right now. The case is closed and so's the door to this cozy love nest, if you follow my drift."

He said, "I'd love to follow you over to yonder sofa, at least. But you did say you have another gent awaiting your return, right upstairs, and I'm not so sure the case is as closed as you think."

She swore, finished her drink, and picked his up, insisting, "I can take more than one of you at a time, you sissy. You ought to see me when the herd's in town. Fess up, you're just too delicate natured for a woman of my nature, right?"

He grinned sheepishly at her and said, "Have it your way if it makes you feel proud. But regardless of how much I might or might not want to go sloppy seconds, the case of Sweet William and Barbara Allan ain't over. Not until I figure out how anyone a heap smarter than she struck me got away with half the things they say she got away with!"

Chapter 12

There were times to go barging in like a bull and there were times to ponder some on one's next move. Longarm ate a solid meal and checked into the Steamboat Springs Palace for some solid shut-eye while all the telegrams he'd sent took their own sweet time running back and forth along the wires. When he woke up again well after sundown his head felt a heap clearer, even before he enjoyed a hot tub, and some hot black coffee in the dining room downstairs. The waitress who served him the java at the outrageous price of a nickel a cup warned him that the kitchen was fixing to close in case he meant to have anything else to eat that night. He was too polite to say he could still taste the apple pie over chili con carne he'd just slept on. He just said he had to get on over to the Western Union and that he'd grab a sandwich somewhere if he wound up hungry after all.

He made it almost all the way to the telegraph office

before he belched, felt how empty that left him feeling, and wondered just where one *could* get a sandwich late at night in a mountain town the size of this one. He considered the kitchen of Kerry Rose, knowing whore-houses served just about anything after dark. Then he warned himself not to dwell on such surroundings, lest he wind up a dirty old man in the end. Like most men who'd ever thought about it at all, he understood the practical advantages of just paying for it and getting off a heap cheaper in the end. But the trouble with being practical about such matters was that, taken to its logical conclusion, a man could save his fool self even more time and trouble in the end if he just stayed home and jerked off. That didn't sound as romantic as even that dumpy waitress back at the hotel. He tried to recall what she'd looked like as he entered the telegraph office. Nothing much came to him. That was just how plain women stuck in a man's brain. He'd know that waitress again the next time he saw her, of course, but had he been required to describe her to another lawman . . .

The reply from Sheriff Blake in Central City proved his point. They'd shown photographic prints of Slats Sullivan and her dead loverboy all around town, making sure even folk too prim to visit the morgue had a look. More than one stickup victim had confirmed that Long-arm had brought down the son of a bitch who'd robbed them. Blake had drawn a blank on old Slats, however. Victims of the outlaw pair only remembered the female as a young redheaded gal. Few had taken time in their moment of sheer terror to admire her looks one way or the other, and in sepia tone with her poor face mutilated so by buckshot, it was small wonder nobody could rightly say whether they'd ever seen her before. Blake said even men who'd laid old Slats in the past had needed some prompting. But the timing fit. Blake reported Squire Tierney had said Slats had been out of town a lot in recent months. She'd told him she had a regular a couple of railroad stops down the line and he'd seen no reason to argue with her, since she didn't get much business at the Peerless in any case. Tierney had also confirmed what Kerry Rose had said about redheaded whores on or about the premises. Blake said Tierney only allowed the whoring to attract drinking and gambling customers and didn't keep close tabs on the soiled doves. But men who paid for it regular recalled Slats being a redhead for a spell, just before she'd suddenly soaked her fool head in stove polish. So, all in all, Longarm was satisfied the two of them had paid, dearly, for robbing the mail stage down from Winter Park that time.

The wire from Billy Vail was shorter and less polite. Vail again demanded Longarm cut the horseplay and get his *Deleted by Western Union* back to Denver if he expected to get paid at the end of the month. He added that he'd told Longarm to do so before Longarm had wired him around noon that Kerry Rose had just too solid an alibi and nobody but the Sullivan gal was left!

Longarm chuckled fondly and tore open the reply from the sheriff's department back in Saint Louis County, Missouri. For the late William Allan was said to have taken part in more than one railroad job with the James and Younger boys, and despite all the blather about Frank and Jesse seeking revenge on the Missouri Pacific Railroad for running over their momma's cat or whatever, the Missouri Pacific simply had no tracks through Clay County, and that famous holdup of the Glendale train had transpired just outside Saint Lou, on the opposite side of the state from their old homestead in Clay County, near Kansas City.

Saint Louis County confirmed that some witnesses

had put William Allan, a.k.a. Sweet William, in the company of Cole Younger about the time of the robbery even though Mr. Younger, currently serving Life at Hard, denied any knowledge of anyone named Allan. They added that the blurry photograph Billy Vail already had was the only known picture of Sweet William, and in case that wasn't enough they once more described the young rascal, as well as anyone could. For aside from his kinky brown hair and heavy eyebrows he'd been a sort of average-looking cuss. Longarm hadn't been astounded by his looks down in Central City, either.

He tore a blank form from the yellow pad on the counter and shot a glance at the Regulator brand wall clock before he blocked out a terse message to his home office. Then he called the clerk over to say, "My boss won't be in his office at this hour, but he'll still be up, at home on Sherman Avenue. That's just up the slope of Capitol Hill from your main Denver office. Can I count on you getting this to him before he turns in?"

The telegraph clerk glanced at the same clock and said, "Depends on when he turns in. I'll instruct the delivery boy to pound on the door whether the lights are on or not. Figure on delivery any time between ten and midnight."

Longarm said that sounded swell, paid cash instead of reversing the charges as usual, and headed back to his hotel. As he entered once more he saw the archway leading into the dining room was dark as the inside of the box they had poor old Slats inside right now, and that reminded him of the coffee sloshing about in his otherwise sort of empty gut. He'd inhaled the coffee so he'd be awake when the night train came through from the west around three A.M., cuss the shipping habits of silver miners in the Great Basin. There'd be peanuts at least in the club car, if it was still open. If he had to, he

166

knew he could last until he got off in the morning. He was just pissed at himself for having to. Had he listened to that waitress before, he'd have ordered more than coffee after just rolling out of the feathers.

On the other hand, he consoled himself as he trudged up the stairs, he didn't have to worry about falling asleep and missing that fool narrow gauge, even if he flopped back down, as hungry as he was already commencing to feel.

He let himself into the room and bath he'd sprung for and hauled the saddle he'd brought over from the livery out of the corner to go through his saddlebags in hopes of finding a chocolate bar or can of sardines, at least. But he'd nibbled like that on the overnight run from Central City and had to cuss himself some more as he gave up and forked the fool saddle over the foot of the bed. He hung his hat, coat, and gun belts, both of them, over a bedpost at the far end. Then he chuckled and took his time stowing the Le Mats in his all-too-empty saddlebags, as evidence. Having fired the fool things in a whorehouse hall he had no desire to repeat the experience. They made great bargaining chips in an argument with assholes, but he didn't fancy a serious fight with such noisy antiques. They'd kicked like mules and created far more of a fuss than needed just to spray so uncertain, next to a real side arm of more modern design. As he buckled them out of sight he muttered, "Sweet dreams, you noisy brats. I wonder why that gal used you to bust her lover-boy out of the lockup at Arnold Wells. You must have kicked even harder in a woman's smaller fists, and all the *noise* was hardly conducive to a discreet getaway. So how in thunder did they *do* that, damn it?"

He didn't expect any answer to his muttering, of course, so he jumped a mite when someone knocked on his hotel door. He grabbed his less dramatic but more pragmatic six-gun from the bedpost as he strode over to the door. He was glad he had the six-gun down at his side when it turned out to be that waitress gal from downstairs. She smiled up shyly at him and held out a tray in her hands as she told him, "I was sure you'd be hungry and, seeing the light under your door, I took the liberty."

He took the tray from her, saying, "Lord bless you, honey, you just saved the window drapes from being devoured by a famished fat head. Come on in while I sit this all down and get out some dinero for you."

She came inside. She even shut the door behind her as she did so. But she stammered, "Oh, I couldn't take *money* for being, ah, sociable. You know what they call women who charge for their favors, don't you?"

He started to tell her she was talking mighty dumb. Then he considered how dumb it might be to do that. For on second glance she had a sweet smile, and her big brown bovine eyes were staring at him sort of wistfully if not downright lonesome. He saw he'd been right in recalling her as neither pretty enough to remember nor too plain to even consider. Her pinned-up hair was thick and healthy enough, albeit a drab shade of pine-bark brown. Her face was almost pretty in the way a plaster window dummy could be said to be pretty. You couldn't make out much of her figure, if she had one, under that shapeless snuff-colored poplin uniform and white apron she still had on. Taking it on faith that she had to be built more loveable than poor old Slats had been, he placed the tray on the bed and invited her to sit on the far side and help him put away all the ham and cheese on rye she'd toted up here with yet another pot of coffee. She protested, "Oh, I couldn't," even though they could both see she'd brought two plates, cups and silver

168

services. He insisted, "Sure you could. If you won't let me pay you, the least you can do is honor me with your swell company, ma'am."

She said her friends called her Tina, and sat down. From the way the mattress moved under her rump, Longarm assumed Tina was short for something more formal, rather than a descriptive term. Calling her fat would have been needlessly cruel. But saying she was tiny would have just been silly. He allowed she could call him Custis and dug in, noting she just nibbled as he got his innards back in shape for whatever came next.

He began to worry some about that as, over a second cup of coffee and sporting pulls on the cheroot he promised never to mention, she commenced to bat her eyelids at him even more obviously. Since she was doing most of the talking, a mite breathless from nerves unless she chattered like this all the time, it developed that as he'd already assumed Tina was a country gal, off a cattle spread even farther from civilization, who'd come to the big city of Steamboat Springs in search of adventure and romance. He'd heard her sad story before. As she moved the tray out from between them, unbidden, and sat down again, closer, he told her in a brotherly way, "If I thought a lot less of both of us, honey, I'd be telling you of the wonders of Denver or, hell, Saint Lou by now. You may as well talk big when you're only talking, and I don't mind saying right out that the temptation crossed my mind, just before that last cup of black coffee cleared it, some."

She smiled uncertainly and said she didn't know what on earth he was talking about. He said, "I figured as much. In sum, Tina, I'm a lawman on a field mission. I've done what I came to do at Steamboat Springs, and so I'll be leaving just this side of three A.M. when my narrow-gauge combination comes through. After that I doubt I'll be back this way soon, if ever. Are you starting to follow my drift, now?"

She nodded, not too brightly, and said, "I think so. You're saying that if we're to make love at all we'd best get cracking lest we not have time to do everything we want to, right?"

He laughed, said, "Well, nobody can say I didn't try, Lord," and hauled her in for a howdy kiss. But even as she wrapped her soft arms around him and pulled him down across the bed with her he just had to warn her, "There's just no way to change the way this all turns out, no matter how much we might want to, honey."

To which she replied by grabbing one of his wrists to plant his hand in her soft lap, pleading, "Don't tease me, then, Custis! They told me downstairs you'd be checking out long before dawn. Did you think I'd take a chance like this with a regular guest?"

He replied, "Well, seeing you put it that way. . ." Then he got her skirts up out of the way and put it in her before she could change her mind or he could wake up.

But he knew the second he slid into her hot hungry tightness that this was no wet dream. She gasped, "Oh, dear, you might have warned me how tall you really were! Don't you think this would feel nicer with all our clothes off, dear?"

It did. She wanted him to leave the lamp lit, too, and as he spread her for full inspection with a pillow under her short-waisted but curvaceous torso he could see why. She had every right to feel proud of her firm young body, and she said she just loved the way his looked, going in and out of her own as she propped herself up on her elbows to watch. He could tell at first entry she'd done all this before, a lot, of course. Yet there was so much innocent barnyard curiosity in her approach to rutting that with her it seemed to be good clean fun. He was even able to tell her, as they were going at it and she complimented him on his staying power, how he'd likely been inspired to these current heights by his earlier visit to Kerry Rose. She didn't act shocked. She seemed to understand how drinking and jawing with a beautiful naked lady for a spell could inspire a man to indecent feelings despite his distastes. As she flattened a cheek to the mattress and arched her spine to take it deeper she sucked in her breath and moaned, "Oh, Lordy, I'm so glad you didn't do this to that other gal this morning, for I just can't seem to get enough of you!"

He told her that made two of them, and he meant it. But later that night, as he lay quietly in bed with another cheroot between his teeth, watching the swell little gal comb and pin her hair back up, he wished they had more time and wondered how come it was always the nice ones, like Tina, a man had to leave behind so sudden.

By the time she'd kissed him and slipped out of his existence as if she'd never been there, tray and all, he figured he had the answer. It was the bad gals, not the good gals, a lawman spent more time and worry on.

Chapter 13

Between changing from narrow gauge to broad, having flapjacks for breakfast in Brighton before changing again, and the infernal Burlington northbound running late, Longarm got into Arnold Wells well after everything was open for business for the day. Yet the backup he'd asked Billy Vail for hadn't shown up, even by nine, and the next train up from Denver wasn't supposed to get there before ten-thirty. So he toted his saddle and possibles over to Regina Morpeth's place before anyone could back-shoot him.

He told the ash-blonde as much when she greeted him at her door wearing nothing worth mention under her smock, with her hair bound up in a kerchief and a feather duster in one hand. He said he was sorry if he'd caught her at a bad time. She hauled him and his things inside, locked her front door after them, and told him there was no such thing as a bad time for him to show up and that she'd missed him just awful.

But as she tossed her feather duster aside and started to slip out of her thin smock, he sighed and told her, "Whoever said virtue was its own reward never packed a badge, I'll vow. Fortunate for me, at least, I ain't as horny this morning as I might have been if I hadn't enjoyed a late snack up in Steamboat Springs."

She took him by one hand to haul him into her parlor as she laughed and asked what on earth he'd been doing in Steamboat Springs, of all places. As they sank down together on a settee and she hauled her smock off over her head, he stared at her regretfully and said, "I wish you wouldn't do that, ma'am."

She shot him a stricken look and covered her naked front with the smock she'd just slipped off, demanding, "Oh? And when did I become a *ma'am* to you again, Custis? Have you forgotten, so soon, what you called me as you took it out of me the last time you passed by, you brute?"

He shook his head soberly and said, "I meant it. You sure screw swell, Miss Regina, and even if you'd screwed me awful I'd still just hate to have to appear in court against you as the arresting officer. So let's talk about how we can best avoid my having to arrest you, shall we?"

She stared at him incredulously. Then she saw he wasn't just making sport of her and rose to turn her bare back to him and slip back into her smock as she asked him coldly, "Just what federal crime do you intend to arrest me on, Deputy Long?"

He told her, "None, if I can possibly avoid it. I suppose I *could* charge you with lying to a peace officer in the cause of obstructing justice, but, like I said, I don't want to sit there like a fool while your lawyer asks how many times I came in you, and where. So I reckon we'd best make a deal, ma'am."

She turned around but remained on her feet, staring down at him as if he'd just sprouted horns and a tail. She licked her lips and tried, "A deal about what, dear? I swear I don't know what you're apparently accusing me of!"

He shook his head sadly and insisted, "It ain't going to work. You already swore you refused to hire room and board to Barbara Allan, Sweet William, and some male confederate. You lied to me, barefaced. The gal known as Barbara Allan never came up here from Central City at all. If she'd had another man to back her play she'd have had no need of my assistance when she decided to get rid of her outlaw lover, not spring him from jail!"

She hung tough. So he quickly filled her in on the deaths of one woman and, count 'em, one man the night before last in Central City. Regina tried, "I never said I saw any of the men she mentioned. If anyone told any fibs it was her, can't you see that, Custis?"

Longarm said, "Nope. You described her too dumb for anyone who'd ever seen Slats Sullivan cum Barbara Allan. You'd *heard* her described and so you just made up enough of a story to throw us all off, and you did. Being female, you suspected any gal with such flaming red hair was likely dying it, so your detail about her needing to touch up her roots was an inspired fib indeed. But fess up, you never laid eyes on the poor ugly mutt, did you?"

Regina gulped and replied, with a nervous laugh, "If you say the real Barbara Allan was ugly, then I must have been taken in by yet some other wayward redhead, Custis. Why would I lie about a strange girl I'd never seen before or since? What point would there be in telling the law such a whopper?"

He said, "We both know the answer to that, ma'am. Why don't you make it easy on yourself and just confirm what I already know? I give you my word I'll only use you as a witness. I can even say you told me, earlier, and that I asked you not to repeat it until I had evidence to go along with our mutual suspicions, see?"

She sobbed, "You're trying to trick me into confessing something I know nothing about, damn you! If you have something on poor little me, why don't you just come out with it instead of playing cat and mouse with me like this?"

He got to his own feet, saying, "I haven't been playing. I'm dead serious. I know you never pulled any triggers. No offense, but your hands just ain't strong enough to fire a brace of Le Mats. I'm even willing to buy it if you want to say you knew nothing about the plot to murder deputies Rice and Trevor. For all I know you didn't. You could have just been asked to repeat a few harmless fibs, maybe in order to nail the lid tighter on that outlaw couple everyone's been after since the Winter Park mail got stopped. Just agree to testify against the polecat who put them big fibs in your sweet mouth and I'll make sure you never serve one day behind bars."

She stepped closer, favoring him with a timid smile as she purred, "Speaking of what I'd like in my mouth, right now, can't we talk about it later, after I've made a man of you some more, honey dong?"

He sighed and said, "I'd like that, too, and you know it. But since I see you've been assured I can't prove anything I reckon I'll just have to go out and prove it. I'll be back once I have, and I hope you'll understand when I have my backup from the district court arrest you. I'd rather not, for obvious reasons, but if you don't want to turn state's evidence, that's the way it'll just have to be."

Then he picked up his saddle, drew the Winchester from the boot, and left with the McClellan braced on one hip and the cocked carbine ready to throw down on anyone who meant to make anything out of it.

The Burlington out of Denver arrived almost four minutes early that morning. Things had to work out that way now and again. There wasn't a soul in sight as Marshal Billy Vail got stiffly down from the train and stared all about, chewing his unlit cigar with the same expression an old pissed-off bulldog might have applied to one end of a bone. A bone with all the juice chewed out already.

As his train rolled on for Cheyenne, leaving Vail alone on the sun-silvered open platform, he growled aloud, "That tears it. You're fired, Longarm. This time you've gone too far, even for you!"

Then Longarm hove into view from where he'd been hunkered among a mess of sunflowers at the base of a water tower. Billy Vail just stood there, seething, until Longarm had joined him on the platform.

Before Vail could cuss his deputy, Longarm snapped, "All right, you dumb old fart, how come you rode up here on your own instead of sending Smiley, Dutch, and maybe Guilfoyle like I asked?"

Vail's bushy brows met in a serious scowl indeed as he replied in an ominously calm tone, "This must come as a hell of a surprise to you, I know, but you don't run the Denver office, Longarm. I do. Where do you get off ordering other deputies into action without bothering to inform your superiors, repeat *superiors*, what in the hell might be going on and who you might be planning to arrest, on what charge?"

Longarm soothed, "I didn't want to put anything that outrageous on the public wire, Billy. You know they won't even let you tell me to fuck myself by way of Western Union. I meant to bring in some mighty serious prisoners with the help of Smiley and Dutch. I've been laying low in the weeds for a while, waiting for them to show up. For Lord knows how I'm supposed to take such desperate sons of bitches alive, alone!"

Vail grimaced and pointed out, "You ain't alone. I just got off the damned train. Who are we after, and I warn you, this better be good. For I sent you to get Sweet William Allan and his doxie, only to have you tear-assing all over Colorado at six cents a mile travel pay, after both Sweet William and his damned redhead were *killed*, you asshole!"

Longarm said, "Sweet William Allan is alive and well, here in Arnold Wells, Billy. The gal that other outlaw held up the mail stage with assured me he'd always answered to Jake. We're still working on who he really was. I left my saddle and Winchester yonder, amid those sunflowers. I'll just go fetch 'em and we'll stroll into town and— Shit, here they come. I figured they'd be looking for me by now."

As Billy Vail gravely regarded the two figures coming down along one side of the railroad tracks from the more settled parts of town, Longarm warned him, "The older cuss with the innocent smile and low-slung .45 would be Cyrus, or Pop, Purvis, the town law. The younger squirt with the strutty stride is supposed to be his deputy, Fred. In point of fact he's really the one and original Sweet William."

Whether it was the loud gasp from Billy Vail or whether they were both experienced gunslicks who knew better than to hold a conversation first, both Pop and his young deputy went for their guns at the same time. Longarm and Billy Vail had been in at least as many shoot-outs, so they were moving sideways, in opposite directions, as they got their own hardware out.

It was still too close for comfort. Vail made the mistake of shooting at the young one instead of the old sneak Longarm had left for him to deal with. So Fred, a.k.a. Sweet William, went down with two rounds in him as Pop Purvis blew Vail's hat off. Then he caught lead from both federal muzzles at once, and still got off an anguished scream or two before he'd finished rolling around on the dusty railroad ballast, dying like a stomped snake by the time the two survivors strolled over for a closer view, reloading as they strode. Vail paused near the sprawled cadaver of the younger one to observe with a worried frown, "I hope you know what we just did, Longarm. This kid don't look all that bushy browed to me."

Longarm kicked the dead man's hat off, exposing close-cropped hair that looked oddly purple in the glaring prairie sunlight. He said, "Anyone can die brown hair, and it's still going to be just as crinkled when he takes his hat off. The brows are simple. Gals pluck their brows all the time, whether they're bushy or not."

Vail demanded, "How come this other son of a bitch wired us they were holding William Allan in their jail if all the time he was posing as one of the damned deputies? None of this makes a lick of sense to me, even though I *saw* the sons of bitches slapping leather on us right now!"

Then he added, "Oh, shit, speaking of slapping leather with the local law..." He had spotted others, some with deputy badges, coming their way on the double.

Longarm said, "Easy does it and let me do the talking, boss. They already know me, and I don't think anyone else was in on it with old Purvis, here. He'd have never needed to murder his own deputies if the whole force was crooked as he was, see?"

At least one of the Arnold Wells lawmen seemed out to prove Longarm's point as he called out, "Thank God we got some real law here at last. What happened to Pop and his nephew, there? We just come running after 'em to tell 'em about Miss Regina Morpeth!"

Vail asked who in thunder Regina Morpeth was. Longarm swallowed hard and asked soberly, "What happened to her?" hoping he might not be told, but not too surprised when the town law told him.

"They just now found her dead, in her own dooryard. One of the neighbors heard a shot, looked out, and didn't see nothing at first. Then Miss Regina drug herself out her front door, crying and bleeding a lot, and by the time anyone could get to her she was gone."

Longarm turned to stare hard at both bodies, muttering, "Some of the loose strings may never be tied up neat as we'd like, now. It's up for grabs which of 'em shot her in a panic, or whether they were out to get us or just catch that train they just missed. Suffice it to say we got all the bad apples accounted for, now. All we have to do is tidy up here, get on back to Denver, and let Henry type it up in triplicate for me to sign, three times. How come you make me do that, Billy?"

Vail said, "Never mind. If you think I mean to wait that long before you explain what just happened, plain and simple, you got another think coming!"

By the time they boarded the southbound, close to sundown after a day spent tidying up indeed, Longarm felt sure he'd explained the infernal story more than once to

Billy Vail's satisfaction, and there was a handsome young gal in a ridiculous hat sitting all alone in the club car, damn Billy's unromantic soul.

But as they sat down a few seats too far from her with their beer schooners, Vail insisted, "The tale is just too convoluted by half, Longarm. Start from the infernal beginning and make me savvy what connection the Sweet William and Barbara Allan in Arnold Wells had to do with the Sweet William and Barbara Allan in Gilpin County, for I'll be switched with snakes if I can see any!"

Longarm sighed, inhaled some smoke, then some suds, and began with, "There wasn't any, Billy. The one and original Sweet William Allan rode with plain old outlaws with names like Cole, Frank, and Jesse. Whether he took part in that disastrous Northfield Raid or not, the gang was badly decimated and scattered by the big mistake they made so far from Clay County."

Vail said, "Neither Frank nor Jesse could be hiding out anywhere near their old homestead right now. It's being watched ferocious."

Longarm nodded, sipped more suds, and said, "That's what I just told you. The Ford brothers have been walking the straight and narrow, but naturally they're being watched as well. So William Allan couldn't hide out with them and may not have even known where the others scattered after they were shot up so swell in Northfield. But Sweet William was neither close kin to the James and Younger clan nor a total orphan. Some of his closer kin and had been halfway converted by the Prophet Joseph Smith during the Mormons' drift through Missouri."

Vail nodded soberly and said, "You already intimated Cyrus Purvis was really related to the rascal he called his nephew, Fred. That would have made Regina Morpeth his kin as well, along with all the Rothbury and Prudhoe folk in town. But if Sweet William fled out west to hole up with long-lost relatives, how did he manage to get himself *arrested* by 'em?"

Longarm inhaled some smoke, then some suds, and said, "He never. Pop Purvis took him in, meaning to introduce him as the fictitious Fred Purvis after Miss Regina did something about his distinctive hair and eyebrows. Females are good at such. But then, refusing to lay low until his kin could lay hold of the hair dye and maybe fake I.D. Pop had in mind, Sweet William went out drinking, overconfident, and Deputy Rice, who was neither kin nor in on it, took a dislike to the young suspicious stranger and discovered a running iron in his saddlebag."

Vail frowned and asked, "How come? Sweet William was a stickup man, not a cow thief, and even if he had been—"

"Rice needed *some* excuse, so he put one in Sweet William's saddlebag," Longarm cut in. "Proddy Bob Trevor's misfortune was that he was on duty at the otherwise empty jail when Rice brought Sweet William in. By the time Pop found out about it his two smart deputies had made Sweet William from the Wanted fliers out on him, and poor Pop had little choice but to go along with their demand he put it out on the wire that they'd captured such a wanted cuss."

Vail nodded and said, "It would have been tough to explain if Purvis had just let the prisoner go. Get to how a fugitive from Missouri ties in with redheaded women robbing mountain stagecoaches with him before he could have got out here. I must confess I find that confusing as hell, old son."

Longarm sipped more suds and explained, "It was confusion Pop Purvis was counting on. We're still working on the true identity of the mad dog an ugly but romantic-natured whore called Slats Sullivan took up with. We do know she preferred to be known as Barbara Allan, from the romantic ballad of the same name. She called her lover-boy Jake. That might have been his name. But as soon as others heard there was both a Sweet William and a Barbara Allan running about robbing folk—"

"They put 'em together, or at least mixed 'em up," Vail cut in.

So Longarm told him, "I'm never going to get to the end of the tale if you keep butting in, boss. Pop Purvis or maybe the poetical Miss Regina had heard or read about Barbara Allan menacing society with a lover-boy noted for bushy brows and Le Mat revolvers. Lord only knows where Purvis found those Le Mats of his own. He could have confiscated 'em off drunken cowhands years ago and saved 'em for a rainy day. He didn't know the outlaw shooting Le Mats down around the gold fields hadn't had his own Le Mats converted to brass. So I began to worry about that as soon as I shot the Sweet William called Jake, down by Central City."

Vail brightened and said, "That's right. You found *brass shells* from a Le Mat *conversion* in that alley across from the jail, but—"

"There you go cutting in again," Longarm cut in. So Vail buried his own face in his beer suds and Longarm continued, "That was more deliberate misdirection, and now you've got me getting ahead of my ownself, damn it. Eating the apple a bite at a time, Purvis commenced by ordering his deputies not to let anyone else in to visit their prisoner. Rice had arrested him after dark, in a smoke-filled as well as dimly lit saloon, and those bushy brows were the only distinctive feature anyone was apt to recall. Having established all over town that

Sweet William was in jail, incommunicado, Pop and Miss Regina spread word about ominous strangers in town, including a gal who sure sounded like that awful Barbara Allan. Then they only had to wait until the streets were clear, at suppertime."

Vail nodded and said, "Right. That's when Regina Morpeth, as Barbara Allan, likely wearing a red wig, busted Sweet William out."

Longarm looked pained and protested, "Damn it, Billy, there wasn't any jailbreak at all. That's how come nobody saw anyone leaving said jail in broad day when they all ran to their doors and windows in response to the dulcet roar of them Le Mats!"

Vail stared owl eyed but silently at him. So Longarm explained, "There was nobody there but Dave Rice, Proddy Bob, and the prisoner. So all Purvis had to do was take Allan from his cell, telling his deputies to just sit tight and he'd be right back with the cuss. Pop Purvis was the boss. Any excuse he gave would have worked as well."

"You mean he just let him go, in broad daylight?" Vail demanded.

Longarm shook his head and said, "Nope. He frogmarched him across to that alley entrance, in case anyone was watching. When nobody was, he just took Allan to Regina Morpeth's house at the far end of the alley for a change of duds and some eyebrow plucking. Then Purvis retraced his steps, dropped some red herring brass in the alley for smart trackers like me to find, and strode into the jail again as if he owned it. His deputies figured he did. So neither was set for a scrap when the boss they both trusted simply whipped out a brace of Le Mats and blasted them dead before they knew what was hitting them!"

Vail started to object. Then he nodded soberly and decided, "Right. By the time anyone else could get

there, Purvis had hidden the murder weapons most anywhere he wanted, it being his own office, and they all
assumed he'd beaten them to the scene of the shoot-out,
having no just cause to suspect him of being the shootist!"

Longarm snuffed out his smoked-down cheroot as he
agreed, "You can't blame 'em for being taken in by
such simple treachery. I was taken for quite a spell,
myself. I might not have ever worked it out if we hadn't
gotten lucky. Nobody planned on the real gal the Barbara Allan nonsense was based on being spotted near
her chosen hideout in the far-off gold fields. Even after
I was miles from Arnold Wells and the real William
Allan, chasing false leads the way a fool pup chases its
own tail, I might never have stumbled over that other
outlaw if his doxie hadn't grown weary of his wild ways
and offered us his head on a plate. Like the real Sweet
William, the one we thought was Sweet William was
laying low, waiting for the heat to blow over and *his*
eyebrows, in point of fact, were only bushy enough to
confuse the issue. He described more like William Allan
than he looked. Had not Slats been killed in all the confusion I might not have ever connected her to the notorious Barbara Allan. Once I did, of course, it began to
add up. Aside from the brass we found in the alley
being all wrong, the Arnold Wells version of Barbara
Allan was all wrong. Miss Regina described her as
cheap and flashy but pretty."

Vail nodded and finished his beer before saying,
"You done well, considering what you had to work
with. It's too bad we didn't get to take any of your
suspects alive. But to tell the truth it may be just as
well. I reckon I understand what you just now said, but
I'd hate to have to explain such a can of wriggly worms
to a judge and jury."

Longarm smiled wryly and replied, "To tell the truth I wasn't looking forward to having to testify against, ah, one of 'em. I did my best to get Miss Regina to confess, but she was too loyal, or too smart, to turn state's evidence. It's just as well for us they didn't know that. Like you just implied, I was going more by educated guess than solid proof."

Vail shrugged and said, "Killing Regina Morpeth, sloppy, and coming at such famous lawmen as us with murderous intent was better than signed confessions. You can always take back a confession in court."

Vail shoved his empty beer schooner away, belched delicately, and added, "It's too bad about the poor little blonde, since her only sin was lying. But it's just as well we'll never have to sell such a shell game to the federal prosecutor. It sure looked as if the escaped outlaw and his redheaded doxie had been brought to justice miles away, and I'm glad Western Union deleted all those mean things I said about you, old son."

Then he rose to his stubby height to add, "My old woman's apt to say mighty mean things if I arrive in Denver tonight with any more beer in me. So I reckon I'll go back to our seats up forward. How about you?"

Longarm indicated the few swallows left in his own beer schooner as he replied in a desperately casual tone, "You go ahead, boss. I may even have another. For I don't have to worry about anyone fussing at me when we pull into the Union Depot tonight. As a matter of fact, I don't have any plans at all for the coming weekend. So unlike your own lucky self, I'll likely wind up lonesome and morose with nobody to tell all my troubles to."

Vail had a wicked little smile on his pudgy face as he eyed the pretty gal sitting all alone under that awful hat, and told Longarm, "I somehow doubt that very much. If

I don't see you no more this evening, make sure you get to the office on time come Monday morning, hear?"

Longarm asked innocently if he didn't always. So Vail warned him not to push it and left.

Longarm didn't turn directly to the strange gal in the even stranger hat. He could see by their reflection in the window glass across the way that she'd already turned to stare thoughtfully at him. He saw she'd been sipping gin and tonic through a straw and that her glass was even more in need of a refill than his. So he got up, moved over to the bar, and got them both refills before he turned around to sit down right next to her. She dimpled at him despite herself and asked if he wasn't taking a lot for granted. He told her he'd noticed she was alone, and said he only wanted to protect her virtue until they got into Denver. So she said in that case it was likely all right for them to protect each other, as long as he promised to keep things platonic. So he promised not to behave at all forward before he'd seen her safe to the big city, and he kept his promise, aboard the train.

What happened after they got to the end of the line is another story.

Watch for

LONGARM AND THE PAWNEE KID

134th in the bold LONGARM series
from Jove

coming in February!

LONGARM

Explore the exciting Old West with
one of the men who made it wild!